Praise for

33 MINUTES

"Readers will be rooting for seventh-grader
Sam Lewis from minute one. Hilarious and heartfelt—
kept me turning pages right to the end."

—Ingrid Law, Newbery Honor–winning author of *Savvy*

"*33 Minutes* is clever and true."

—Amy Ignatow, author of *The Popularity Papers*

"Great fun! A fast-paced story filled with humor and heart."

—Alan Silberberg, Sid Fleischman Award–winning author of
Milo: Sticky Notes and Brain Freeze

"A rollicking and heartfelt adventure.... Come for the fun.
Stay for the Tater Tots."

—Evan Kuhlman, author of *The Last Invisible Boy*
and *Brother from a Box*

Check out these other Aladdin MAX books!

The Last Boy at St. Edith's

I Am Fartacus

Under Locker and Key

Coming soon:

The Wild Bunch

Todd Hasak-Lowy

33 MINUTES

Illustrated by bethany bARTon

ALADDIN MAX
NEW YORK LONDON TORONTO SYDNEY NEW DELHI

ALADDIN MAX

Simon & Schuster Children's Publishing Division

1230 Avenue of the Americas, New York, New York 10020

This Aladdin paperback edition April 2017

Text copyright © 2013 by Todd Hasak-Lowy

Interior illustrations copyright © 2013 by Bethany Barton

Cover illustration copyright © 2017 by Andy Smith

Also available in an Aladdin hardcover edition.

All rights reserved, including the right of reproduction in whole or in part in any form.

For information about special discounts for bulk purchases, please contact Simon & Schuster Special Sales at 1-866-506-1949 or business@simonandschuster.com.

ALADDIN and related logo are registered trademarks of Simon & Schuster, Inc.

ALADDIN MAX is a trademark of Simon & Schuster, Inc.

The Simon & Schuster Speakers Bureau can bring authors to your live event. For more information or to book an event contact the Simon & Schuster Speakers Bureau at 1-866-248-3049 or visit our website at www.simonspeakers.com.

Cover designed by Laura Lyn DiSiena

Interior designed by Hilary Zarycky

The text of this book was set in Sentinel.

Manufactured in the United States of America 0717 OFF

2 4 6 8 10 9 7 5 3

The Library of Congress has cataloged the hardcover edition as follows:

Hasak-Lowy, Todd, 1969–

33 minutes / by Todd Hasak-Lowy. — 1st Aladdin hardcover ed.

p. cm.

Summary: An epic lunch period leads to a fateful showdown as small, skinny seventh grader Sam's former best friend—now a popular athlete—promises to beat him up at recess in exactly thirty-three minutes.

ISBN 978-1-4424-4500-0 (hc)

[1. Middle schools—Fiction. 2. Schools—Fiction. 3. Friendship—Fiction.]

I. Title. II. Title: Thirty-three minutes.

PZ7.H26865Aam 2013

[Fic]—dc23

2012009604

ISBN 978-1-4424-4500-0 (hc)

ISBN 978-1-4814-8995-9 (pbk)

ISBN 978-1-4424-4502-4 (eBook)

To Noam

Much Thanks To:

- Dan Shere, Joey Garfield, and Josh Lewis, for ideas and encouragement.

- The Dawes Boys-to-Men Book Club, for savvy feedback and an excuse to eat a Morgan Sturtz Special.

- My impossibly wonderful daughters, Ariel and Noam, for expert commentary and the desire to write for the not-yet-adults of this world.

- Simon Lipskar, who, even though this isn't your book, helped me see it needed some last-minute surgery.

- The always reliable and absurdly knowledgeable Daniel Lazar, for ushering me into the world of children's literature and for making this book better in endless ways big and small.

- The deserving-of-a-cape-and-chest-logo-all-her-own Liesa Abrams, for giving this book a home, understanding exactly what it still needed, and making me want this to be just the first of many, many books we work on together.

• Taal, for making it so I can write in the first place.

33
MINUTES

11:41 A.M.

"Think about this: Had the British not won the French and Indian War," Mr. Griegs says, "we'd all be speaking French right now."

Fact: I am in social studies.

My hand goes up. I'm not sure I want my hand to be up, but too late, it's up.

Fact: I am the smartest person in social studies (although some people would say that's only my opinion).

Sometimes Mr. Griegs ignores me, because I have this "nasty habit of getting us off topic." But he's feeling generous today. He tosses a piece of chalk from one hand to the other, catches it, and points at me. "Hmm. Sam Lewis wants to make a contribution. Well, out with it."

I try to act like I don't know the answer to my question. "Well, um, do you really think, Mr. Griegs, that we'd be here at all right now if they hadn't won?"

Fact: Laughter.

Mr. Griegs, all eleven feet of him, considers this for a moment as he chews on his mustache. Then he crosses his arms. "Explain, Lewis."

Interested heads are turning toward me, because this is what happens when you're me and you sit in the back of class and talk a lot and sometimes annoy the teacher. "Well, there is a story called 'A Sound of Thunder' that I read because my dad thought I'd like science fiction, which I sort of do." Mr. Griegs and his mustache make his "please get to the point" face, which involves him pausing his mustache snack while rolling his eyes and shaking his head, so I try to hurry up. "A group of hunters go back in time, and one of them accidentally steps on a butterfly—that's the only thing he does—and when he gets back, all sorts of things have changed, like who the president is, just because of that one butterfly. This would be much more than a butterfly, don't you think?"

Mr. Griegs starts munching on his mustache again, uncrosses his arms, and puts the chalk in his pocket, where he'll probably forget it. Some days by the end of class he's got four or five pieces in there. "Yes. Probably. So?"

Opinion: Mr. Griegs thinks the most important thing he can teach us is to tell the difference between facts and opinions. He often says things like, "That's just your opinion" and "It is an *indisputable* fact that. . . ." He gets very excited whenever he catches one of us mistaking an opinion for a fact. He points his finger at the offender (his long arm reaching halfway across the classroom), beams like a mad scientist, and says, "Aha!" Mr. Griegs is hardly my favorite teacher—in fact, he pretty much stinks—but sorting things between fact and opinion can make boring classes less boring (and there are plenty of those here), so I guess he's not all bad.

"So then, I don't know, maybe we wouldn't be sitting here right now. Maybe there wouldn't even be social studies then."

Fact: Most of the class is now giggling and/or exchanging high fives.

"Keep it down." Mr. Griegs takes a couple long, long steps toward us as he raises his voice. "That's enough." He looks right at me, not very pleased. "Okay, Lewis. I get it. Very clever. How's this? It was a pretty"—he pauses, nibbles on his facial hair, and scrunches up his face—"*decisive* war."

"Okay," I say, shrugging my shoulders and regretting that I put my hand up in the first place.

Mr. Griegs's eyes light up all of a sudden. "And I'm sure, Lewis, that you know that this decisive war started over the meeting of the"—he snaps his fingers and brings his lips together, pretending not to remember something—"what were the names of those two rivers again?"

I straighten up a bit in my chair. "The Allegheny and the Monongahela?"

Mr. Griegs turns his back to the class, takes a couple

slow steps toward the board, but then twists around quickly, with a scary smile on his face. "And those two rivers, Lewis, in what city do they meet?"

I grip my pencil tightly and focus on his mustache. "Uh . . ." Mr. Griegs's smile continues to grow, because he definitely never told us this. Lucky for me, maybe, my parents have a road atlas in the back of their car, which I like to study sometimes. "Pittsburgh?"

Mr. Griegs's face is way more red than it was a minute ago, but he won't give up. "And what river do those two rivers form?" He's smiling again, because he's foolish enough to think he's about to humiliate me, even though it's April 12th, meaning he's been my teacher for eight months already, meaning he should know better by now. "Well, you do know which river they form, don't you, Lewis?"

I really don't want to do this to Mr. Griegs, since it will only make him want to humiliate me more later on, but what choice do I have? "The Ohio River," I say sort of quietly, "Mr. Griegs."

I'd never tell this to anyone or anything, but it might be

a fact that I am actually the smartest person in my school, though, obviously, some people would say that this, too, is only my opinion.

Fact: Scattered giggling.

Not that being smart is always such a good thing.

Mr. Griegs's whole face (his eyes, nose, mustache, and mouth) shrink down into an angry dot. Sometimes I wonder if his face isn't made out of rubber, because a normal person's face can't do half the things his does.

ANGRY

EXCITED

HUMILIATED

IMPATIENT

VICTORIOUS

IN SPACE

I look over at Amy Takahara, who smiles at me a little.

I don't know if I would call us friends exactly, but I will say that whenever she smiles at me, or even near me, especially lately, my stomach acts like I'm at the top of a giant roller coaster. She's "the new girl," or at least was at the beginning of the school year. I would guess that she has never spelled a word wrong in her entire life—plus, she has perfect penmanship. Or pengirlship.

One day back in October, Mr. Griegs wrote "bucaneer" on the board, and then I heard Amy start squirming, even though she normally sits completely still. I looked over and saw her flipping quickly to the back of her notebook, where she wrote, *October 17th: bucaneer, buccaneer.* This page is now about ninety words long, because Mr. Griegs isn't a particularly talented speller. Around Thanksgiving, I passed her a note that said, *Why don't you correct him?* Her eyes got quite large when she read it. I got a note back that said, *NO WAY!!!!* She underlined "no" about nine times.

Not that I'm a big fan of passing notes these days.

There is still some giggling coming from the front of the

class, where Morgan Sturtz sits. I think I can make out his laugh, which comes from the bottom of his chest and sounds like "*huh*-huh, *huh*-huh, *huh*-huh." But I can't be sure, because he sits exactly three seats in front of me, because we used to talk too much during class at the beginning of the year, so Mr. Griegs moved Morgan. He's not a very good speller, especially when it comes to vowels.

Opinion: The problem with the whole fact/opinion model is that it isn't always so simple.

Because when Morgan Sturtz said I was a "big jerk" yesterday, well, that was clearly just an opinion. But when the three other people there definitely agreed, then at what point does that become a fact?

Mr. Griegs recovers from his "decisive" defeat at the meeting of history and geography (ha-ha, aren't I funny?) by reminding us who's in charge and making everyone hate me at the same time: "Fine. Next Monday's test will now be this Friday."

Fact: Most of the class says, "Ugh."

Opinion (maybe): I am going to get my butt kicked in exactly 33 minutes.

It is hard to say whether a statement about the future is a fact or an opinion. It's obviously not a fact, because it hasn't happened yet. But then think about this: Yesterday Morgan Sturtz told me, to my face and with three witnesses nearby, "I am totally going to kick your butt tomorrow at recess." His face was so red when he told me this that I was almost worried about him (and not just about myself and my butt).

Morgan is (fact) ten inches taller and forty pounds heavier than me, not to mention the best athlete in the school (two-thirds fact, one-third opinion). Plus, I'm the worst athlete I know (fact, not opinion, trust me). Plus, I know Morgan very well, because we (fact) used to be best friends, so I know (confidently held opinion) he wouldn't make a threat like this if he didn't plan to carry it out.

Then isn't his kicking my butt pretty much already a fact?

Fact: The bell is ringing.

32 minutes.

11:45

Walking alone through the somewhat clean halls of Wagner Middle School, even when I have just over a half hour to live, helps me gather my thoughts.

For instance:

Why would anyone even say "kick your butt"? Yesterday evening, not long after Morgan screamed out his plan to kick mine (I was already on my bike, pedaling ten times faster than normal), I searched for some sort of explanation on the Internet. Only I came up empty. But I really did want to find out where this phrase first came from, because when a person screams something like, "Go ahead, Sam, run away. Doesn't matter, because I am totally going to kick your butt tomorrow at recess. I'm serious!" this person is actually saying, *Sam, I am going to hurt you very badly.*

And so if that's what he meant, then "kick your butt" is a weirdly nice way of putting it. Because if you knew someone was going to kick you some place, would you not hope for that place to be your butt? The butt is, after all, the most padded location anywhere on your entire body. Consider other places and how much less you'd like them to be kicked: hand, shin, armpit, stomach, face, and, uh, a certain very sensitive region.

I really, really hope there is no kicking of my certain very sensitive region.

The walls of our fine hallways are half covered with posters, because this is someone's idea of interior decoration. I pass one that looks like this:

The halls are filled with hundreds of my fellow Wagner Middle School Vikings. Many of them are looking at me with unusual interest, elbowing each other, whispering, and, all in all, having fun at my expense.

Because there are no secrets in middle school when it comes to the future kicking of butts.

But here's the thing about that STOPS poster: Morgan isn't a bully. He has not kicked any other butts in the time I have known him. No, he's simply very, very, very mad at me. And maybe he should be. This is different from bullying, which, according to Principal Benson (a few months back he called a mandatory nine-hour "Say No to Bullying!" assembly), is a stronger person (the bully) taking advantage of a weaker person (the bullied) over and over.

I can't rule out the possibility that Principal Benson forcing a marathon "Say No to Bullying!" assembly on us is an example of bullying. Because if giving him my lunch money would have made him stop blabbering, I would have happily emptied my pockets.

Meet my locker: 28-13-21. Open says me. Hello and welcome to the smell of all the lunches I've ever stored here, especially the one and only egg salad sandwich I ever allowed my somewhat concerned mother to pack into my lunch box. And because that's not bad enough on this already bad day, just two lockers down is the one belonging to Chris Tripadero, the jerk partially responsible for the transformation of Morgan from my best friend to someone who will, very soon, kick my butt or, more likely, punch my face.

Chris moved to our neighborhood a couple summers ago. I remember, because a few days before the start of sixth grade there was a knock on our front door, so I went to see who it was. There was Chris, playing with his iPod Touch, and his dad, Mr. Tripadero, wearing a fancy suit even though it was Saturday.

"Hello, I'm Bob Tripadero," his dad said with his hand sticking out toward me, "and this is my son, Christopher."

"Hi, I'm Sam," I said, shaking his hand and looking over at Chris, who didn't even look up from his game.

"Sam"—Mr. Tripadero grinned like he was trying to sell me something—"I was hoping to speak to your mother or father. I don't suppose either of them is home?" Next thing I knew, they were in our kitchen.

Turns out that Chris was going to be attending Wagner too, only Mr. Tripadero leaves for work really early every day and is actually out of town a lot, so Mr. Tripadero wanted to know, "I was wondering if it might be possible for me to drop off Christopher at your house each morning, so that he and your son [he probably already forgot my name] could walk to school together?"

"Of course," my mom said with a friendly smile, offering Mr. Tripadero coffee and Chris some cookies. And sure enough, thanks to her generosity, Chris was dropped off on our doorstep at 7:15 a.m. two days later.

At first it wasn't so bad. He was the new kid, so I could explain stuff to him and he'd almost listen (even though we were both new at Wagner, so I didn't really know any more about this place than he did).

"That's Capital Drugs," I told him that first Monday on the way to school. "It's closer than QuikPik over on Middle-belt. But they don't like kids because they always think we're just trying to shoplift stuff. Plus, candy bars are cheaper at QuikPik."

"Whatever," Chris said, almost laughing. "I never get caught."

Chris had about a thousand games on his iPod—plus, he usually gave me part of the breakfast he brought with him, which most of the time was two packets of Pop-Tarts, the super junky kind my parents never let me have.

Soon we were kind of friends, even if he didn't talk too much and showed up half the time without a backpack, wearing the same shirt he had on the day before. But then I made the mistake of inviting him over one day when Morgan was coming over too. Because then they became friends, which was okay at first, because at least we were all three friends. Plus, I was better friends with both of them than they were with each other.

But then that all changed. All of it.

"Lew [because he calls me, or used to call me, Lew], we should totally start hanging out at Chris's house," Morgan told me almost a month later while we were watching stupid videos on YouTube. "That place is sweet."

"You've been to Chris's house?" I asked while some guy who was trying to do a flip landed on his head and almost knocked himself out.

"Yeah," Morgan said, cracking up at the poor guy on the screen. "It's *huge* inside. Like a mansion or something. I swear."

"When were you at his house?" I still hadn't been there.

"Last Sunday," Morgan said, like it was no big deal. "Oh, wait." He started typing something. "Have you ever seen the one where the guy trips into his pool? It's hilarious!"

The whole thing looks something like this:

FRIENDSHIP FLOW CHART

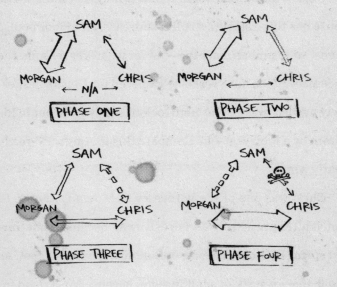

Chris sees me now, even though I'm trying to remove my lunch silently while hiding my head behind the open locker door. But lockers clank and jangle, because schools are where everything is stupid. He smiles at me. And even though his gruesome smirk has nothing in common with Amy Takahara's magical smile of four minutes ago except for the word "smile," my stomach again does something it shouldn't.

"Hi, Sa-am," Chris says, like he's trying out for a job at a haunted house.

Chris's disastrous version of a family has money. His house has three stories, a spiral staircase, an indoor pool, a sauna, and a pinball machine—but for whatever reasons, the necessary funds have yet to be gathered for Chris's desperately needed braces. His teeth look like they were put in his mouth by a four-year-old. Compare this to Amy's TV-ready pearly whites.

Chris was one of the witnesses to Morgan's threat. In fact, it all happened on Chris's driveway, because sometime last spring his house became our unofficial hangout spot. As usual, there wasn't an adult in sight, because Mr. Tripadero is a "consultant" and spends most of his time in Singapore, Malaysia, and the Philippines (this according to his dangerous son, who definitely cannot be trusted). I'm guessing

Mr. Tripadero is really an international spy or a successful criminal. All I know for sure is that a lot of the time Chris is the only person in his house, since his mother lives in New Jersey and his older sister has already escaped to college.

I'd tell my parents all this if they actually cared. But what can I do, since they like to say, "As long as you keep your grades up, you can be as independent as you want"? So then what? I need to act stupid for them to care about me?

"Hi, Chris." I'm not sure I said it out loud.

Bad things happen in Chris's house. Things like finding rock-hard dog poop from one of their yapping poodles in the deep shag carpet in the corner of the living room. Or seeing darts floating in the fish pond they have *inside* their house. Or watching, from right up close, a bowling ball fall from a third-story window to the driveway below without anyone yelling anything like, *Hey, Sam, look out, we're about to drop a fourteen-pound bowling ball out this window, which we know is stupid, but you gotta admit that throwing a fourteen-pound bowling bowl out a third-story window is pretty cool, so, you know, heads up and all that.*

"Lunch, Sam-Sam. And then recess!" Chris is very happy. In addition to his teeth, his skin is much closer to green than most people's.

But they didn't say anything, so the ball landed about five feet from me. I really don't think they were trying to kill me. I really don't. But I felt new cracks in the asphalt form under my feet, not to mention the sweat suddenly pouring out of every inch of my skin and totally soaking my clothes, which (the sweat) somehow kept flowing for at least ten minutes even after I realized I wasn't going to get crushed by a fourteen-pound bowling ball dropped out of a third-story window. There are probably scientists employed by deodorant companies who could explain why sweat acts this way. As for me, just one more source of confusion.

I shut my locker and turn away from Chris, even though the lunchroom is right past him and he knows it.

He's really, really good at cackling.

11:49

If some evil person wanted to make the Wagner Middle School cafeteria an even louder echo chamber, could such a person find a single change to make? The walls, the floors, the tables, the trays, the heads of the students inside: hard, flat, cruel. Yes, I know, those are (supposedly) sound-proofing tiles up there on the ceiling, but I'm not fooled. Because the moment you step inside this rotten mealtime cavern, you may as well be at a jackhammer convention.

Cafeterias are the scariest places on earth, because no one should ever have to eat in the same room as 450 other people, unless the food is super yummy, which (duh) is not the case here at Wagner Middle School.

First part of previous statement, opinion. Second part, fact. Trust me.

Not to mention the smell, which is like my locker, if:

- you could stand inside it with the door closed
- it held ten thousand times more lunches, including a large number of egg salad sandwiches gone bad
- the lunch smell had been locked in a thirty-year-long battle with the stink of cleaning supplies that are showered down on the tiling of the cafeteria floor each afternoon.

End result: combo bleach-and-tuna-fish air freshener.

Not to mention, things got even worse this year, when some committee of child-haters came up with the "Eat Right!" campaign. Meaning now we have to survive a half hour inside this giant feed-hole five days a week without the comfort of a Twinkie or a Ho Ho. Now the words "lunch" and "cream filling" have nothing to do with each other. Now sixth-grade nostrils go to work on baby carrots like massive junkyard magnets on scrap metal.

The cafeteria somehow stinks less when you have friends to sit with. But I have been standing just inside the entrance to the cafeteria for the last thirty seconds, paralyzed, unable to locate a place to *not* eat my lunch (because of the unpredictable nature of my coming butt kicking—which could actually be a stomach punching—I have decided that keeping my gut empty would be wise). My old table is now out of the question. Things between Morgan and me have been not so great for months, but as late as last Friday, I could still sit near the edge of our group and down the contents of my insulated lunch box.

Not anymore.

Just this last September, me and Morgan were still together all the time. Or at least a lot. He was over at my house on the weekends, his playbook filled with *X*s and *O*s opened up on our living room floor, while I helped him memorize plays. My dad, if we could drag him out of his study (we usually couldn't), would be quarterback. We'd find a bunch of other stuff—pillows, pots, my microscope, shoes, our toaster, the big bin of LEGOs Morgan and I used to play with—and set it all up as the other players. Morgan, of course, would be the running back, the O behind the quarterback. I'd line up on the other side as middle linebacker, the X in the middle (or "$X - 4$," as I liked to call myself, a joke Morgan would have gotten if he hadn't stopped caring about math the year before; he actually used to be pretty good at math until he started putting on that stupid helmet of his, which is supposed to protect his head but seems to have turned off his brain instead). Then I'd call out a play, so we could check if Morgan remembered where he was supposed to go for each one.

So I'd scream something like "East H-24!" and my dad (or, more often, QB LEGO Bin) would hike the ball and hand it to Morgan, who would try to remember if he was supposed to go right or left, if he was supposed to run between the vacuum cleaner and the rocket launcher or the laundry detergent and the solar-powered car I made that one afternoon he told me he couldn't go to the movies. Then I'd tell him "yes" or "no" as I pretended to try to tackle him. Sometimes I'd grab on to his legs and let him drag me across the soft carpet all the way to the dining room, because I think Morgan thought that was a good drill for him.

Players O and X – 4 would practice like this for an hour or more, Morgan getting it right very, very, *very* slowly. But I didn't mind. I wanted him to get it right—I really did—plus, it was the closest I'd ever get to being his teammate. Sometimes I wished there were some way he could help me with the ArithmeTitans, but other than trying to learn to put on that calm, confident expression he puts on along with his uniform before games, there wasn't much he could teach me. Though it wouldn't have hurt if he ever acted like he cared about all the points I was scoring too.

I'm still looking for a place to sit when I notice the single worst thing about this very, very bad cafeteria, the thing that makes me think that whoever is in charge of this whole place doesn't like us kids very much: the Wagner Middle School salad bar. Look, overall I have nothing against the idea of salad. Lettuce is not necessarily evil, especially when used in the construction of a hamburger. But a whole bowl of the stuff? Not to mention, this has got

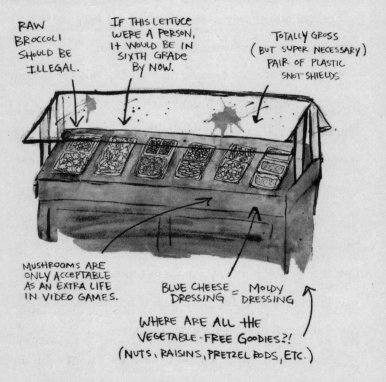

RAW BROCCOLI SHOULD BE ILLEGAL.

IF THIS LETTUCE WERE A PERSON, It WOULD BE IN SIXTH GRADE By NOW.

TOTALLY GROSS (BUT SUPER NECESSARY) PAIR OF PLASTIC SNOT SHIELDS

MUSHROOMS ARE ONLY ACCEPTABLE AS AN EXTRA LIFE IN VIDEO GAMES.

BLUE CHEESE DRESSING = MOLDY DRESSING

WHERE ARE ALL THE VEGETABLE-FREE GOODIES?! (NUTS, RAISINS, PRETZEL RODS, ETC.)

Not to mention, this very sad salad bar is situated in the space where the powers that be could just as easily offer a hot pretzel stand or (it hurts even to think about it) a soft-serve ice-cream machine.

Oh, soft-serve ice cream, will you ever forgive us?

But today—scanning the evil cafeteria over and over, hoping to find shelter—I notice the one person capable of saving Vegetable Central: Amy Takahara. And she sees me.

"Hi, Sam!"

She smiles again, so my stomach, already trained to report to duty upon arrival in the cafeteria, does an extra loop. I wave, in part to keep my balance. She motions for me to come over. My legs seem to think this is a good idea.

I am standing opposite Amy Takahara, who, thanks perhaps to her East Asian genes, is one of four seventh graders at Wagner Middle School shorter than the thirteen-year-old me. Next to Amy is Caitlan Phillips, who will one day play professional softball, unless there isn't such a thing. Caitlan is definitely *not* one of the other members of the munchkin patrol (she's probably taller than me on her knees).

Amy jabs me with one of her elbows. "Sam, you were so funny today with Mr. Griegs."

Caitlan and her all-star overbite ask, "What'd he do?"

Another jab. "Yeah, tell her what you did."

I'm trying to look at Amy and not at her plastic bowl of nutrition, but I fail. On top of her lettuce is a pile of a dozen or more chickpeas, each coated in a snotlike film.

I close my eyes and say, "I can't believe you have the audacity to eat chickpeas."

"You talk so weird, Sam. But yeah, I *lo-ove* chickpeas." Amy more or less sings this.

"Plus," Lady Softball adds, "they're packed with antioxidants."

I know a lot of things, but antioxidants are not one of them. The confused look on Amy's face tells me that she has no idea either. Which doesn't mean she couldn't spell it correctly anyway.

Amy taps my bag with the edge of her tray. "What are you having?"

I make another survey of the cafeteria, but no luck. "For lunch?"

"Yes, silly"—another jab, perhaps to get my attention— "for lunch."

I turn back to her, trying to avoid another glimpse of those chickpeas. "I don't know, but I'm not too hungry."

"Why not?" Amy appears very concerned.

"No reason," I say, like it couldn't have anything to do with me getting pummeled soon.

At which point Caitlan leans in (and way, way down) to whisper something to Amy, even though I'm standing right there. Her lowered torso gives me a clear view of students exiting from the hot lunch line at the far end of the cafeteria.

"No, I don't believe you," Amy says in a half whisper.

Caitlan shrugs. "That's what everyone's been saying."

"Sam, is it true?" Even more concern on her perfect face.

And I'm about to answer when Morgan steps out from the lunch line.

11:53

Of course, it's the second Monday of the month.
Chicken patty sandwich, tater tots, and applesauce. A carton of 2 percent milk. The perfect pre-fight meal, or, to be more precise, pre-demolish your ex–best friend meal. Some protein, some carbohydrates, and a healthy dessert to keep you light on your toes.

Morgan's always had a soft spot for the chicken patty. Like my love for its fishy friend (next Friday, if I'm off my all-liquid diet by then). He will have politely requested an extra packet of ketchup, as he is to ketchup what Amy (so sad, I want to cry) is to chickpeas. After sitting down, he will construct the Morgan Sturtz Special.

how to
MAKE
the MORGAN STURTZ
—SPECIAL—

x1
CHICKEN PATTY
SANDWICH

x2
KETCHUP
PACKET

x6
TATER TOTS

STEP 1:
REMOVE THE TOP
HALF OF THE BUN
FROM THE SANDWICH.

STEP 2:
OPEN ONE (1) PACK
OF KETCHUP & SQUEEZE
IT OUT ALL OVER
THE PATTY.

STEP 3:
TAKE 5 OR 6 TATER
TOTS AND PLACE THEM ON
THE CIRCLE OF CHICKEN.

STEP 4:
OPEN THE SECOND PACKET
OF KETCHUP AND SQUEEZE
ITS CONTENTS ALL OVER THE
NEWLY RELOCATED TATER TOTS.

(LOCKS
IN THE
FLAVOR!)

STEP 5:
RETURN THE BUN TO ITS
ORIGINAL POSITION & SMUSH
THE SANDWICH DOWN TO
A BITEABLE HEIGHT.

*NOTE: THE MORGAN STURTZ SPECIAL SHOULD
BE CONSUMED IN 45 SECONDS OR LESS.

31

"Hello?" Amy's small hand is waving in front of my face. "Earth to Sam." Amy is standing by herself. Caitlan must have gone off to consume her full day's supply of anti-oxidants. "Is it true?" She's definitely not smiling.

"Is what true?" I say, watching Morgan make his way toward what used to be our table.

"That you and Morgan are going to fight after lunch." She's moved right in front of me, trying to cut off my view.

I look back at her. "The term 'fight' suggests that I might take an active role in what's about to happen."

"C'mon, I'm serious, Sam."

If I had to bet, I'd put money on the fact that Morgan is an inch taller than he was yesterday afternoon. Hard to be sure, since he's halfway across the cafeteria, but it definitely looks that way. Which only makes sense. I've never been bigger than him since we met in first grade, but over the last year he's grown about a foot, or at least way more than I've grown. Six inches, eight inches, ten inches—all I know is the part of Morgan in charge of making him grow has been working overtime. Meanwhile, the part of me that's supposed to do the same still hasn't reported for duty. Maybe it was hanging out with the part that does long division and got distracted. If you happen to see it, do me a favor and tell it to get to work already.

"Sam, you can't fight Morgan." Amy speaks very slowly, emphasizing each word.

I stare at her for a second and think about begging her for help. Instead, I say, "If you mean I can't beat Morgan in a fight, you're pretty much stating the obvious."

"No, I mean you guys are *friends*." She stresses this word. It hurts to be reminded. "Friends don't fight."

"*Were* friends, Amy," I tell her, trying to sound matter-of-fact about it. "We *were* friends. Ex-friends do fight sometimes. Like, oh, I don't know, today at recess."

And then, even though he's already passed us, Morgan turns his head and looks right at me. My stomach, apparently overworked already, doesn't respond. Instead, my knees wobble, and I'm thankful it's not me holding a tray full of food.

"What happened?" Amy asks, sincerely worried. I'm

grateful for her concern, but life was easier, or less difficult, when I was focusing on the simpler problem of where to sit. "Why aren't you friends anymore? He was your best friend."

In addition to all my other areas of expertise—algebra, cell biology, the basics of HTML code, to name just a few—I know everything there is to know about Morgan's facial expressions. I know, for instance, that when Morgan brings his eyebrows together while flaring his nostrils, he's angry, but if he only brings his eyebrows together, he's just determined. I know he tends to bite his bottom lip and squint his right eye a bit whenever he's really concentrating on something he's not very good at, like recalling if *H* means "go to your right" in the Wagner Middle School football playbook. And I know he'll show his teeth when he's really happy, because when Morgan smiles with just his lips, he's just trying to be polite.

I shrug, eyes on Morgan. "Friends come and friends go, Amy, what can I say?"

Only now, even from halfway across the cafeteria, I can tell that no amount of searching my Morgan Sturtz Facial

Expressions Database will produce any results. Because his face is totally blank. No anger, no confusion, no nothing. But he's not looking through me either, he's looking right at me. He's taking step after step, twisting his head ever so slightly in order to keep his eyes locked on me, but I can't for the life of me figure out what, if anything, he's trying to tell me.

Amy nudges me with her tray. "No, but you guys were best, best friends. That doesn't make any sense."

Could it be he's trying to figure out what *my* face is saying?

Fact: I have no idea what it's saying right now, unless it somehow knows how to say, *Please don't hurt me. Please be my friend again.*

Amy turns her tray to the side in order to take a half step toward me. "Do you want me to talk to him? I will, if you want."

And then she smiles again, offering me for the third time today the kindest facial expression in the Detroit metropolitan area. Because it's right across from me, because she got up the nerve to make it just for me, knowing

I would know it's just for me, I realize I'm allowed—no, I'm *supposed*—to look at it: her smile, her round cheeks, her warm, smart, perfect-spelling eyes. Amy Takahara knows I might be bleeding all over the playground in twenty-four minutes, but she still likes me.

Amy. Takahara. Likes. Me.

So I see her, no, I see her *and* me, in my living room, no, in *her* living room, in her family's sensibly furnished living room (even though I've never seen her family's sensibly furnished living room). I'm lying on their fancy leather couch, or maybe the reclined La-Z-Boy, their walls tastefully decorated with Japanese calligraphy prints or even just ugly paintings by Amy's mom. And there's Amy, gently placing an actual raw steak over my brand-new black eye. She'll stick by her man, Amy will, even if he's still pretty much a boy.

Too bad she's a vegetarian. Could tofu work like steak when it comes to black eyes? And didn't I recently read you actually shouldn't put a steak on a black eye? And what if it's more than a black eye? What if she doesn't really believe there will be a fight at all and won't like me after, whether or not I lose badly or just lose, because Amy's a pacifist who doesn't even eat fish?

What if the last perfect smile she ever gives me is this one, right here in front of the salad bar?

Morgan sits down in his spot, right next to Chris, who's sitting in what used to be my spot. Seeing them together is more than I can handle, so I turn my head away, only to spot Mr. Glassner passing by the entrance to the cafeteria.

"Look, Amy, I gotta go."

11:56

A voice, from above: "And where do you think you're going?"

Mr. Griegs and his mustache. He doesn't just teach social studies, he monitors the cafeteria.

I look up, way up. Need to think of something. Why not the oldest excuse in the book? "The bathroom."

Mr. Griegs has never worn an article of clothing that fits him even a little bit. Today's pants need to be seriously let out in an area let's call the "just below the belt" region. I notice this unfortunate fact since my eyes are opposite his belt (which now boasts an impressive walkie-talkie).

He shakes his head very slowly back and forth. "Oh, no, you're not."

I raise my head a bit more. "But I really need to go."

Mr. Griegs crosses his arms and tilts his head to the side, like we've been through this a dozen times. "What you really need to do is wait for the end of lunch, Lewis, just like everyone else."

If it wasn't bad enough that I have to get past a gatekeeper in order to escape, my neck is now getting sore, because I have to look straight up to make eye-to-mustache contact (the alternative being a lowered head and just-below-the-belt contact). And if I know my fellow Vikings even half as well as I think I do, then a bunch of them have already noticed our standoff, Mr. Griegs's crossed arms and downturned mustache announcing a confrontation.

The time to act is now. Unlike Morgan, Mr. Griegs doesn't scare me.

"Mr. Griegs, I need to visit the restroom. This is a fact. If I do not visit the restroom very, very, *very* soon, something pretty bad will happen. Something along the lines of the"—I pause to take a deep breath—"the Reagan Moody Incident." Mr. Griegs's mustache trembles at the very mention of the Reagan Moody Incident, which led to a special emergency meeting of the PTA. "It's up to you, Mr. Griegs."

Mr. Griegs uncrosses and recrosses his arms, because he thinks slowly. Next he removes his walkie-talkie and checks one of its dials. "You think you're pretty smart, Lewis, don't you?"

I try not to smile, which today is pretty easy. "I think I need to go to the bathroom, Mr. Griegs. That's all."

Mr. Griegs's mustache appears to twitch. "Go on." He raises half his upper lip, like he just figured out how bad it smells in here. "Get lost."

I hurry out of the cafeteria, hoping to catch Mr. Glassner, if only because he's always on my side. More and more, that leaves him pretty much all by himself.

You see, I understood when Morgan decided to watch

the Michigan–Michigan State game instead of coming to the Novi Math Olympics Invitational. At least I tried to understand. Even though I skipped the ArithmeTitans' preseason pizza meeting to watch one of his stupid scrimmages.

But I didn't mind missing the pizza meeting. Not that much, anyway. I didn't even mind when Morgan skipped the Novi Invitational. Okay, I did. But not too much. But I did mind what he did (or didn't do) at the assembly the next Friday.

That was the day of the annual fall pep rally. In other words, the annual football rally. Fine, I know people care about football about four thousand times more than they care about math, even though football isn't responsible for us having cars or computers or cell phones. But Principal Benson was considerate enough (or maybe dumb enough) to mention the ArithmeTitans at the beginning of the rally, since we won the Novi Invitational the weekend before.

With the entire student body in the bleachers (except for Morgan and the football team, who all stood next to him in their jerseys), Principal Benson announced, "Before introducing our brave Gridiron Vikings, I would like to take a moment to recognize another Viking team that scored an impressive victory last Saturday. Our very own ArithmeTitans, led by"—he looked down at his notes—"led by Samuel Lewis, captured the Novi Invitational for the second year in a row. How about a big Viking round of applause for the ArithmeTitans!"

I was actually sitting next to Amy that day, because I didn't know who else to sit next to, because I sure wasn't going to sit next to Chris without Morgan there. Amy gave me a big smile and started clapping loudly. But she was one of only about five people not allowed in the teachers' lounge applauding. All five of whom stopped when, a couple seconds later, Chris yelled:

At which point everyone laughed. Except Amy and (most of) the teachers. Everyone including Morgan.

I told my parents about it that night, even though I wasn't planning to. It was Mexican Fiesta Night at our house, and everyone was passing around the salsa and the sour cream and the guacamole when suddenly it just came out. They said they were sorry, and then they looked at each other for a while, like they had figured out how to talk to each other without opening their mouths. So I pretended I needed to put more cheese on my taco. Then my mom wiped her mouth with her napkin—which she does a lot, even though I've never seen any food stuck to her lips—and said, "I'm sure Morgan didn't really mean to laugh. It was probably just nervous laughter."

Then this weird smile took over her face. A weird smile that could have meant anything other than her being happy. A weird smile that I bet meant she didn't really believe that he didn't mean it. I almost was going to say something, but I didn't, because what good is her lying some more going to do? So I just picked up my taco and kept eating.

Where is Mr. Glassner?

11:59

Hoping to find Mr. Glassner, I turn a corner and hurry down the math hallway. He's nowhere to be seen, but then:

"One thousand four hundred forty-four!"

Mr. Glassner, from somewhere behind me and down the hall.

I turn around and pause before answering, because somehow it's more impressive that way. "Thirty-eight."

"Thirty-eight. Let's see." He's walking toward me with his small, tight steps, in his trademark double-breasted blazer, since there's a meet today.

That's right, there's a meet today. They had to reschedule. How could I forget? Hmm, must be something else on my mind, I can't imagine what. Just my luck to have to miss a meet because of injuries to the butt. Or to the face. Or to the stomach. Or to the everywhere.

"Carry the six . . . twenty-four . . . that makes . . . Right again, Mr. Lewis, right again."

After the square root established itself as the coolest of all mathematical symbols in our Tournament of Most Awesome Mathematical Symbols, Mr. Glassner bet me my own personal pizza party that I couldn't memorize all the whole square roots up to one hundred.

"Are we ready to strut our stuff against E. C. Dunbar Middle School's finest today?" Mr. Glassner, as usual, is smiling. Smiling because he always smiles, smiling because he's talking with the strongest math student in the school— and captain of the ArithmeTitans, thank you very much—

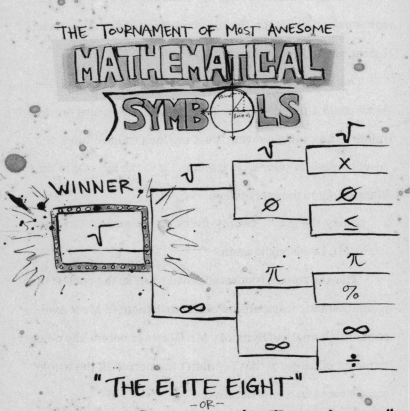

THE TOURNAMENT OF MOST AWESOME
MATHEMATICAL
SYMBOLS

WINNER!

"THE ELITE EIGHT"
—OR—
"THE TERRIFIC TWO to the THIRD POWER"

smiling because it will be his pleasure to pay for those pizzas

if I keep up my end of the deal (which he knows I will).

Mr. Glassner has tiny eyes set far back in his head, the kind that make you wonder how he sees. And when he smiles, which, again, is all the time, they're even smaller.

He is my favorite person in this building over the age of fourteen. And yes, I know, nothing boosts your popularity at middle school like being good friends with someone born in 1962. Nothing except being captain of the ArithmeTitans.

I shrug my shoulders. "Sure, I guess."

Mr. Glassner actually stops smiling for a moment. Long enough to ask, "Is everything okay?" Then, back to smiling.

"I'm fine, sure." I try looking into Mr. Glassner's eyes, both because he's one of about two teachers here who deserves it and because I can't help but try to find them (his eyes) each time I talk to him. His eyebrows naturally point up at a nearly forty-five-degree angle, which, combined with his endless grin, gives him this cheery "well, what do you know?" expression at all times.

"Remember my friend from U of M? The professor I told you about?" Mr. Glassner is extra tickled by this question.

"The math professor?"

Extra-large smile. "That's the one!"

"What about him?" I ask Mr. Glassner.

He raises his eyebrows, super excited by what he's about to say. "Does the phrase 'special celebrity judge' mean anything to you?"

I ask Mr. Glassner, "He's coming to today's meet?"

"That he is! Officially to judge, but secretly"—Mr. Glassner leans in to share with me his widest smile yet—"to see our brightest star in person." He points a friendly finger at my chest. "You!"

Mr. Glassner leans back a bit, dials his smile down to a huge grin, puts his hands in his pant pockets, and begins rocking back and forth on his toes and heels. "There are, you know, summer university programs for students like you, Sam. Places where you can rub elbows with the other whizzes of your generation. Professor Davies sits on the advisory board of one such program. A good showing today, Sam, and you'll be a shoo-in. He told me as much."

It's not that I don't like being an ArithmeTitan. I do—a lot, even. *Survive recess* and *Be able to compete today* would be two of my three responses if someone gave me three wishes right now (*Be friends with Morgan again* would be the other one, the first one). But I only joined last year to begin with because I got sick of Morgan being gone at football practice all the time. I couldn't help being good at it, and then, I don't know, I didn't mind being great at it. I wanted to be great. I still do.

But Morgan seemed to mind, which wasn't fair. I mean, c'mon, I couldn't tackle him if my life depended on it, but I still helped him learn his plays. So he's not so great at math anymore, big deal. So he decided playing football is more important than studying, whatever. Why couldn't he quiz me on geometry theorems anyway? Why did he have to laugh with everyone else instead?

"Five thousand one hundred eighty-four!" Mr. Glassner's eyes are almost wide with excitement.

I try to act like I'm taking some pleasure in this. "Seventy-two."

"Right again! At this rate you ought to start putting together your guest list for that pizza party I'm going to owe you. No question, Sam, you've got what it takes"—he pauses (waiting for me to join in, which I do, almost enjoying it) as we say together, our fists in the air—"to be an Arithme-Titan!"

"Now off to lunch with you," Mr. Glassner says. "You can't very well find x on an empty stomach." And he starts down the hall again, one tiny step at a time.

He's right, I ought to get back to the cafeteria before Mr. Griegs sends out a search party.

I'm almost back to the cafeteria when Marc Quigley, the most humongous eighth grader of them all, steps out into the hallway and starts heading toward me. I try not looking at him as I slowly drift to the opposite side of the hallway, which shakes every time one of his size eighteen shoes crashes down on the floor. Marc Quigley doesn't have a reputation for being a bully or anything, but how close would you get to the massive foot of a supposedly calm elephant?

Even though the tiling feels like it's turned into a trampoline, I pass by Mount Quigley without injury. My nose, however, wonders what in the world has gone wrong, because Marc Quigley isn't just humongous, he's humongously stinky. Like he's got a year-old bacon cheeseburger glued under each armpit.

Maybe that's where the problems began.

Because there was that day at the Tripaderos' last summer. We were on Chris's roof—me, Morgan, and Chris, along with Jordan Gutman and Brandon Berk. Throwing things, but not bowling balls, at all the trees nearby. The Tripaderos' house has a flat roof, and the place is surrounded by tons of tall trees, so all in all, it's not such a bad activity. Our parents may not have liked that we were throwing shoes and apples and canned goods and not, say, small rocks, but there weren't any adults around. In fact, my parents didn't seem to care much where I was going in the first place, so they definitely didn't get a vote.

The object of the game was to hit the trees with the stuff. The farther the tree, the bigger the stuff, the louder the impact, the better. After we ran out of shoes, apples, and

cans of tomato paste, Chris went inside and returned with a
duffel bag packed with new ammo: dog toys, CDs (which
required a Frisbee-like toss and led to a separate game),
candles, batteries, and, of course, lightbulbs.

IN MEMORY:
STUFF SACRIFICED
AT HURLAPALOOZA

4 APPLES   2 ORANGES

3 CANS OF
TOMATO PASTE

YOU WERE
GOOD AT
BEING D
FATHERS.
♡ SAM

1 CAN OF
BAMBOO SHOOTS

2 LEMONS   20 CDS

11 DOG TREATS

1 CAN
OF TOMATO
SAUCE   12 LIGHT
                                BULBS

8 D BATTERIES

6 AA BATTERIES

14 CANDLES

5 SHOES   2 ROLLS OF PENNIES

3 DOG TOYS

HERE LIE the
MOST TOSSABLE
HOUSEHOLD
PRODUCTS.

Morgan quickly emerged as our most skilled and fearless marksman (Chris was our most fearless, and generous, supplier). He kept hitting tree trunks straight on, and one time he actually lodged a thick D battery inside the soft bark of the tallest tree. The competition eventually turned into a performance by Morgan for the rest of us (except for Gutman and Berk, who disappeared to the other end of the roof with a stack of twenty recordable CDs).

Despite some shade from all those trees, the sun was blazing on the roof and we had all worked up a sweat, especially Morgan. Before starting on the lightbulbs, saved for last, Morgan took off his white shirt and tossed it behind us, where it landed on some sort of thin, metal chimney. So I went over to remove Morgan's shirt, since that chimney looked like the kind of thing that could tear something. I picked up the shirt, which smelled alive, and noticed two dark yellow stains, one in each armpit.

The lightbulbs, even the heavy fluorescent ones, were a bit of a letdown. Either too light to throw hard or too hard to break against a tree. But Morgan gave it his all just the same. By the end he was dripping sweat, and the muscles in his arms and across his chest and back were huge from the effort. Chris cheered him on the whole time, not caring that we were literally throwing his family's things away. But me, I was definitely ready for something else, because how long can you watch Chris watching Morgan hurl stuff? I went inside, visited one of their three upstairs bathrooms, and waited for them to get bored.

When I went back out there (I waited around inside for ten minutes before finally giving up), the other four were on their backs, all shirtless, looking up at the sky. Berk was spinning the last remaining CD on the tip of his finger, and a bright reflection caught me straight on. Chris welcomed me back by joking obnoxiously, "I hope you left some toilet paper for everyone else."

Then Morgan said, "Lew, where the hell have you been? Get over here already."

So I got on my back, shirt still on, next to Morgan. Chris asked how many bathrooms I used, but I didn't say anything, silently thanking Morgan for thwacking Chris in the chest and telling him to stop being a dweeb. Morgan stunk, and I wanted to ask him about those yellow stains.

Instead, I got up, found an extra-large flashlight battery we had somehow missed and a flip-flop peeking out of the duffel bag. "Hey, guys," I shouted. "Science experiment time."

"Science experiments suck" was the quick response, but I didn't give up.

"C'mon," I said, "if we drop them at the same time, which one will hit the driveway first?"

Chris sprung up first and begged Morgan to launch the battery at the tallest tree. Gutman and Berk, meanwhile, had their eyes on the flip-flop, which they thought would give the last CD some good competition in a final toss-off from the other end of the roof. But Morgan, who still took my side from time to time back then, said, "Shut up, you guys. Lew, what are you talking about?"

Morgan took the battery from me, held it in his hand, getting a sense for its weight. It was heavy enough to cause Morgan's bicep to bulge noticeably. The flip-flop weighed almost nothing. "The battery, duh" was his verdict, and the others fell in line behind him.

I announced, trying to say it as if I had just thought it up, "I think they might hit at the same time." They cackled, so I asked, trying to sound like I wasn't sure I thought this was a good idea, "Anyone want to bet?" They all gave each other high fives, and a minute later we had settled on Slurpees. Four for me if I won. One for each of them if I lost. Berk and Gutman ran downstairs to judge from the driveway.

Me, Morgan, and Chris walked toward the edge of the roof, with me holding both objects. I'm not scared of heights, but I'm not *not* scared of them either. When we got near the edge, I felt a hand push me on the back. Not hard enough to send me over, just hard enough to terrify me. Chris cackled once more, so I asked him, "Do you always have to be a total idiot?"

Chris said, sneering, "Maybe I like being a total idiot."

I didn't answer Chris, but Morgan said, "C'mon, Chris, cut it out."

Chris murmured, "Who cares, he's buying me a Slurpee soon anyway."

Gutman and Berk ran out onto the driveway, Berk flashing us with the disc to signal their arrival. They counted to three together. I let go. The objects hit at pretty much the exact same time, of course. I tried not to gloat, I really did, but when I turned to Morgan, I couldn't help showing my satisfaction at having performed a successful experiment. He used to tell

me I was awesome when one of my experiments went right.

PHYSICS IS PHUN!

GALILEO GALILEI (SUPER AWESOME ITALIAN GENIUS FROM WAY BACK) PROVED THAT ALL OBJECTS FALL AT THE SAME RATE, EVEN IF ONE IS REALLY HEAVY AND THE OTHER IS PRETTY LIGHT.

WHEEEE!

FLIP-FLOP

MEGA BATTERY

HE DROPPED STUFF FROM THE LEANING TOWER OF PISA JUST TO MAKE SURE.

(EVEN THOUGH IT'S NOT TRUE, YOU SHOULD TELL ALL YOUR FRIENDS HIS MOST FAMOUS EXPERIMENT WAS DROPPING A WATERMELON AND A BALLOON FILLED WITH SPAGHETTI SAUCE AT THE SAME TIME.)

WATERMELON

BALLOON FILLED WITH SPAGHETTI SAUCE

(BUT YOU SHOULD <u>NOT</u> TELL YOUR PARENTS YOU GOT THE IDEA TO DROP A WATERMELON AND A BALLOON FILLED WITH SPAGHETTI SAUCE FROM <u>ME</u>.)

Morgan looked extremely confused. "You knew, didn't

you?" Extremely confused and more than a little upset.

"Maybe," I said, half smiling, half not smiling, half wanting to smile, half not wanting to smile. A year earlier he would have been totally into the experiment. He even would have listened to me talk about Galileo afterward. Well, at least I was smart enough to keep my lecture to myself up there on that hot, smelly, stupid roof.

Chris and the others were all making noise about something, but I ignored them. Morgan definitely looked hurt. "You knew," he said again, shaking his head.

"Yeah," I said, and then maybe I did mumble something about Galileo. I guess I couldn't help myself.

"Galileo." Morgan lost his patience. "Who the hell is Galileo?" But before I could answer, he said, "Why do you always gotta be showing off?"

This is what Morgan "The Hurler" Sturtz wanted to know.

Why was *I* showing off? *Me?* Did Morgan really say that? Like I was the only one showing off. I couldn't believe he was actually serious.

But he was.

I never even bothered collecting on my Slurpees.

12:05

The only thing worse than walking into the
Wagner Middle School cafeteria once each day is walking
into it twice, like I've had to do today. For some reason, it's
way louder now than when I left. I swear I can almost see
the noise.

Thankfully, Mr. Griegs has left his post in order to super-
vise the cleanup of what looks like a three-student pileup a
few feet from the salad bar. Pat McDonald, Armin Dervy,

and some girl in pigtails are trying to rebuild their lunches—
two hot, one packed—scattered nearby. Mr. Budds, our nine-
hundred-year-old janitor, is taking detailed directions from
Griegs, because everyone knows that sweeping and mop-
ping are difficult tasks.

A sudden uproar comes from the darkest, dirtiest, noisiest
corner of Lunchland, also known as The Place Extremely
Weird and Socially Challenged Sixth-Grade Boys Eat.

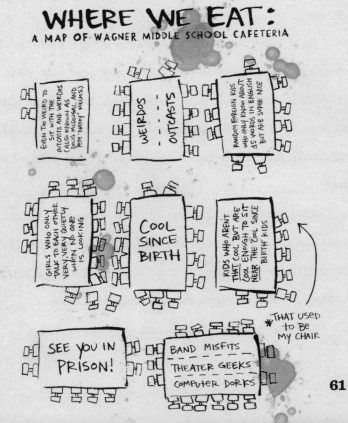

WHERE WE EAT:
A MAP OF WAGNER MIDDLE SCHOOL CAFETERIA

EVEN TOO WEIRD TO SIT WITH THE OUTCASTS AND WEIRDOS (ALSO KNOWN AS DOUG MUDDFAL AND PETE "NATTY" HELMS)

WEIRDOS

OUTCASTS

RANDOM FOREIGN KIDS WHO ONLY KNOW ABOUT 45 WORDS IN ENGLISH BUT ARE SUPER NICE

GIRLS WHO ONLY TALK TO EACH OTHER VERY, VERY QUIETLY WHEN NO ONE IS LOOKING

COOL SINCE BIRTH

KIDS WHO AREN'T THAT COOL BUT ARE COOL ENOUGH TO SIT NEAR THE COOL SINCE BIRTH KIDS

* THAT USED TO BE MY CHAIR

SEE YOU IN PRISON!

BAND MISFITS
THEATER GEEKS
COMPUTER DORKS

My eyes track down the source of a high-pitched laugh-shriek combo: Benny Fink, an amusing runt who lives down the street from me, is being dragged up, over, and across a table by two of his "friends." These "buddies" are using my neighbor's underwear as a handle. Benny, laughing uncontrollably, seems to be enjoying the ride. Mr. Griegs senses this new development and rushes off to squelch it, covering the distance between the two crime scenes in four enormous strides.

"Sam! Sam! Sa-am!" I finally hear Amy's voice break through the fog. Somehow she is standing right next to me.

"Oh, hi. Sorry. I ran into Mr. Glassner." But she's already walking away from me, then turning half around and quickly motioning for me to follow her. She has a serious look on her face.

I sit down next to Amy and much too close to her chickpeas and greens. My lunch box (which I've been holding for most of the last ten minutes in my sweaty right hand) is not happy to be sharing the table with actual vegetables.

"He's super mad at you." She isn't smiling.

"Who?" I ask this only because I'm not sure I really feel like talking about it.

"Who." She rolls her eyes. "Morgan, you doofus."

I open my lunch box out of habit. "And you think I didn't know this?"

"I mean super, super, *extremely* super mad." She sticks her plastic fork into her bowl. "But he wouldn't tell me why."

"Did he say if he still plans to kick my butt in"—I look up at the cafeteria clock—"nine minutes?"

She takes a bite of salad and chews a bit before answering. "No. But a bunch of the other guys, Chris and Brandon and Jordan and Kyle and some other jerks, they sure seem to think he is. They think it's funny."

"I know." I move the contents of my lunch around. PB&J, chips, grapes. All headed to the garbage.

"Sam"—Amy's so concerned, she puts her fork down next to her bowl of antioxidants—"what happened between you two?"

I think this is what she just asked, and I'm thinking

about answering. I'm thinking about telling her any and all of the following:

- All he wants to do is play sports.
- He thinks all I want to do is schoolwork and study tenth-grade math.
- But I still wish he wanted to come over more.
- And my parents barely seem to notice that he barely does.
- Plus, there's that really stupid thing I did that's really to blame for today, that's so stupid I can't even say it out loud.
- I just want us to stay friends.

But I don't say anything because I'm not even sure that's what she asked in the first place, because at that moment the decibel level in the Wagner Middle School cafeteria finally reaches rock-concert level. I look up and see that Armin and Pat have started a game of floor patty, which quickly inspires copycat competitions, with at least a half dozen chicken patties now gliding across the waxed floor. Meanwhile, the underwear-as-handle fad has quickly spread among the rest of the sixth-grade boys and whoa, a sixth-grade girl as well.

"Oh my God," Amy sums up the situation nicely.

Mr. Griegs runs around the cafeteria like a chicken with its head cut off, assuming this headless chicken somehow has a fuzzy mustache and a pair of four-foot-long rubber stilts where its legs should be. Through the noise, I think I can hear him shouting into his walkie-talkie, "We have a 9–18 situation in the cafeteria, I repeat, 9–18 in the cafeteria! This is not a drill! 9–18!! 9–18!!!" Janitor Budds, meanwhile, takes one of his many daily breaks, sitting on the edge of the cafeteria stage with a toothpick between his gums.

Amy and I, being both short and curious, stand up on our bench to get a better look. We try to continue our conversation, even though the cafeteria keeps getting louder and louder.

"So what happened between you two?!" she screams into my ear. "I thought you guys were best friends!"

Phillip Gruden, Wagner Middle School's leading theater dork, is juggling three chicken patties while singing a show tune.

I lean toward her, keeping my eyes on the chaos every-where. "We were! But we started fighting a lot!"

Poor Benny Fink is wearing the back of his underwear over his head, like a hood. Actually, Poor Benny Fink looks perfectly happy being Poor Benny Fink.

"Fighting?!" she screams.

At the end of our very own table Ashley Rorshack, Wagner Middle School's all-time leader in giggles per hour, stands helpless as two crooked streams of 2 percent milk flow from her eighth-grade nostrils.

"Arguing!" I explain loudly. "Having disagreements!"

A heroic sixth grader lunges for Mr. Griegs's undies.

"Why?" she hollers back.

My old table, though not actively engaged in any full-blown mischief, eggs on their fellow Vikings, except for Morgan, who stands with his arms crossed and considers the mayhem in silence.

I turn to Amy and open my mouth, only I don't know where to begin.

Because is there really any way you can explain to someone how me and Morgan went from the guys who won our first-

66

grade field day competition together to the guys who are going to fight in eight minutes? How can I even get her to understand what that day at Deer Creek Elementary was really like?

Picture this: It's the end of our kickball game against the second graders, a game everybody had been talking about for a couple weeks already, like it was the Super Bowl or something. Last inning, two outs, no one on base, score tied. Sam Lewis steps up to the plate. I crush the ball (yes, that's right, *I* crush the ball) over Kenny Telurski's head and make it all the way to second. Next up? Who else but Morgan Sturtz. Morgan connects with the big red ball, but not quite as hard as he wanted. But so what, I just start running, because I can run pretty fast, at least I could back then. Jason Briggs (bigger in second grade than I am right now) is waiting for me at home, waiting for the ball to tag me. But guess what? I beat the ball and score. I score the *winning* run.

We won, we won because of me, because of me and Morgan. I was the hero and so was Morgan, and everyone was jumping up and down and slapping us on the back, and when we sat down for ice cream after that, I knew we just became best friends. I just knew.

Somehow the feeling of that day turned into the feeling of that summer and the feeling of second grade, and third, and fourth, and even fifth. Like we weren't just best friends, we were the best, period. The best whenever we were together. And so we always were. My mom used to call us "MorSam." But then MorSam got here, to this stupid school, and something changed, everything changed, changed in a way that was bigger than football or math. Until next thing I know, MorSam's annual Friday-after-Thanksgiving tradition (Morgan comes over that morning and we take every last toy in my room and build two massive armies that fight all day long) turns into a five-minute joke that ends with Morgan going downstairs to watch football with my dad, who doesn't seem to think anything is wrong at all.

How do you explain any of that?

I look at Amy and shrug my shoulders.

And then it takes a moment for me to realize what I'm seeing: A milk carton whizzes past Amy, missing her head by no more than an inch.

12:08

Some questions about food fights:

Why don't they happen every day? Why aren't there weekly food-fighting activities at our local community center? Why isn't there a television show called *The Wonderful World of Food Fights?*

Ever since I was really little, my mom would try to distract me whenever I was really upset about something. I'm crying, and suddenly there'd be a giant jigsaw puzzle on the kitchen table, or she'd pull out a bunch of ingredients and ask me if I wanted to help her make her super yummy oatmeal-walnut-chocolate-chip cookies, or she'd say, "Hey, Sammy, let's go through your clothes and see what you've outgrown since the summer" (she'd say this even though I still fit into the Lions sweatshirt I got for my tenth birthday).

So here's what I want to know: Why didn't she just start chucking cupcakes at me? Because right now I feel like I don't have a problem in the world.

The great thing about food fights is that even if you throw some food at somebody and miss (which is obviously the case with me), you still get to throw food at somebody. It's a win-win situation. Plus, sometimes, like when you're Mandy Berlin with a sidearm delivery, you can miss but still hit a much better target, in this case a gangly school teacher/monitor who now has a yogurt-covered mustache. Unless that was her target all along, in which case, Ms. Berlin, you are my hero.

Plus, I wasn't going to eat my lunch anyway.

Amy enthusiastically approves. Just one more entry in

the "yes" column on the "Is Amy Takahara Totally and Utterly Awesome?" sheet.

Though the chicken patty would seem to be the center-piece of today's hot lunch, food value is measured differently in Foodfightaville. In Foodfightaville tater tots are an 8.3 (out of 10) on the tossability scale (they lose some points for being too light), while applesauce scores a 9.7 in splatability. Which isn't to say that people aren't heaving their chicken patties with everything they've got.

FIRST TIME IN A FOOD FIGHT?
NOT SURE WHAT to THROW?
JUST GRAB ONE OF THESE CLASSICS
AND YOU CAN'T MISS!

TOSSABILITY
SOFT-BOILED EGG 9.9
BABY CARROTS 9.2
STRING CHEESE 8.8
(NON-CHEWY) GRANOLA BAR 8.5
TATER TOTS 8.3

SPLATABILITY
CLAM CHOWDER 10
APPLESAUCE 9.7
FRUIT-AT-THE-BOTTOM YOGURT 9.4
CHOCOLATE PUDDING 9.2
SPAGHETTI AND MEATBALLS 8.9

STICKABILITY
GUM (FRESH OUT OF YOUR MOUTH) 9.7
PB&J (MUST REMOVE THE JELLY SLICE) 9.6
LOLLIPOP (see GUIDELINE FOR GUM) 9.4
HOT-LUNCH NACHOS 9.2
FUDGE 9.0

Not to mention that the cloud of noise from before has turned into a full-blown fireworks display, because this is beyond fun, this is beyond the "hey, that was great" fun of a good movie, an afternoon of laser tag, or even a trip to an amusement park. Because this isn't good, clean fun—this is bad, messy fun, which reminds me and every other applesauce-coated Viking here of all that naughtiness they've kept us from since we were old enough to understand what naughty was. This is exactly *not* why they have places like Wagner Middle School in the first place.

Kids are laughing and shrieking and whooping and hollering and barking and jumping on one another and rolling around on the ground and using trays as shields and wearing bowls as helmets and crawling with their hands in their shoes and attempting to swim freestyle through a pool of ranch dressing.

I turn to Amy, who has just sent her chickpeas back toward the salad bar (where they belong). Her hair has mustard highlights, and next thing I know, we're high-fiving each other but then not letting go of each other's hand. After at least 2.7 seconds of pure joy, Amy pulls her hand back, extends a stubby, condiment-coated index finger, and runs it along the skin between my nose and my mouth, because giving someone a combination ketchup–ranch dressing mustache is a sign of friendship in many places around the world.

Energized by this show of affection, I leap from our bench and head through the flying lunches toward Morgan's table. Because maybe a not-so-little food fight is all Morgan needs to get over his silly grudge.

I walk slowly and confidently in his direction. I am pelted with more foods than you'll find in aisles three through eight of your local supermarket. But I do not care one bit.

Each and every door to the cafeteria is now opening, with every single teacher pouring in to answer Mr. Griegs's urgent 9–18 call. Mr. Rozier, the mightiest chemistry teacher this side of the Mississippi, has just tackled a half dozen tater-tot-armed eighth graders who had lined three sixth graders up against a wall. Ms. Ruyak, our hefty PE teacher, is blowing her whistle and herding students into a corner.

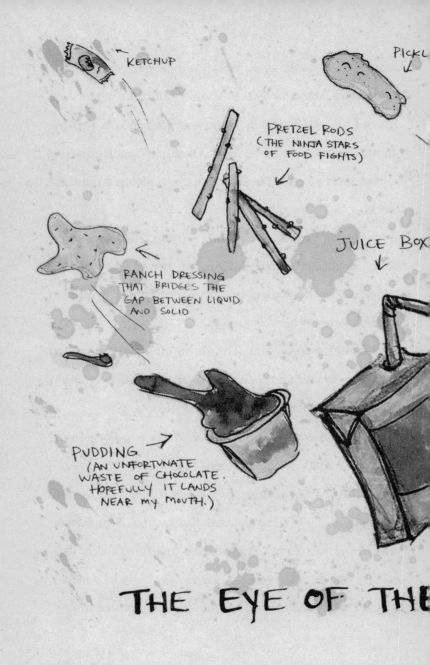

KETCHUP

PICKL

PRETZEL RODS
(THE NINJA STARS
OF FOOD FIGHTS)

JUICE BOX

RANCH DRESSING
THAT BRIDGES THE
GAP BETWEEN LIQUID
AND SOLID

PUDDING
(AN UNFORTUNATE
WASTE OF CHOCOLATE.
HOPEFULLY IT LANDS
NEAR MY MOUTH.)

THE EYE OF THE

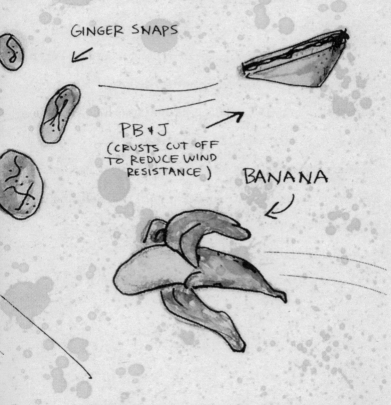

STRING CHEESE →

PIMENTO LOAF
(BECAUSE YOUR
PARENTS HATE YOU)

GINGER SNAPS

PB&J
(CRUSTS CUT OFF
TO REDUCE WIND
RESISTANCE)

BANANA

OOD STORM   12:11 P.M.

But right now I don't care about anything other than getting Morgan to smile back at me. I stride toward him, I hold out my arms, I tell him with my eyes, *C'mon, pal, if all this can happen, then anything can happen, then even the two of us can make up and be MorSam like we used to be.*

Amy calls out to me, so I quickly spin around.

But she's just pointing ahead, quite concerned. When I look back toward Morgan, I notice, definitely a moment too late, that some fool over at his table has decided that the heavy-duty salad bowls are fair game too.

And then something hits my head, hits my head hard, and I start spinning. Spinning fast, until the table and the kids and all that food are just one big blur.

And then things get really weird.

12:16:37 TO
12:16:46

Ladies and gentlemen, welcome to the battle of the century!

In this corner, standing at five feet, five inches and weighing one hundred twenty-two pounds, hailing from Glenn Hills, Michigan, future Division I college athlete and babe magnet extraordinaire, Morgan "The Factual Opinion" Sturtz.

And in this corner, measuring four feet, seven and

five-eighths inches and tipping the scales at almost eighty-four pounds, also hailing from Glenn Hills, Michigan, master of math, brightest star in the standardized testing galaxy, and future king of the nerds, Sam "The Square Root of Puberty" Lewis!

Well, Jim, the waiting is finally over. This one has all the makings of an instant classic. The Factual Opinion, undefeated in his last eight showdowns, has announced that if he wins, he'll donate half his sweat to charity. Meanwhile, the nearly dangerous and hardly imposing Square Root of Puberty has countered with an offer to tutor underprivileged children in pretending like you can't smell unbelievably stinky eighth graders in public if he survives this match.

That's right, Bob, and in addition to a lifetime supply of Slurpees and tater tots, the winner of today's fight will receive an all-expenses-paid trip to Washington, DC, to see Amy Takahara compete in the eighty-sixth annual Scripps National Spelling Bee, where she will also be a scholar-in-residence at the Institute for Adorable Smiling.

And here she is now, Jim, right at ringside, the always

fetching and punctual Takahara, offering to display the placards announcing each round along with one of this week's vocabulary words. I for one sure hope we make it to round eight. It's been much too long since I've seen "audacious" printed up in big letters.

Now let's go over to Mr. Griegs's mustache, which spoke to both fighters just moments ago.

Well, guys, The Factual Opinion was all business outside his locker room. He said he's going to focus on the *i*-before-*e* rule and not saying hi to Sam in the halls when other guys from the team are around. Meanwhile, The Square Root of Puberty told me he plans to go out for third-string punter while posting on the Internet excerpts from Morgan's C– book report on George Orwell's *Animal Farm*, which, The Square Root of Puberty added, is a pretty good grade considering The Factual Opinion read only the first four and a half pages of it.

Now, fighters, you know the rules: No purposely misspelling words when the other is cheating off your quiz; no picking the other last; no correcting the other in social studies class; no "forgetting" to invite the other to your birthday party; no blaming farts on the other when girls are around; no biking so fast up hills; no getting impatient when explaining to the other what the Golgi apparatus does; no pretending your new PlayStation doesn't work; no saying you're going to dress up for Halloween and then laugh when the other one comes over dressed up like a mobster and accidentally used a permanent marker for the stubble; no saying your mom didn't give you the message; no tackling hard in Kill the Guy; no inviting the guys over for cards and using a marked deck; no not saving the other a place; no spreading the rumor that the other thought the Civil War was between the United States and Germany; no not sticking up for the other when oversized eighth graders like TJ Potts purposely bump into him outside Mr. Glassner's room; no not offering to split the last one; no canceling a sleepover and then going to someone else's house; no explaining being dropped off at Kim Cohen's party together by saying it's just because your moms are friends; and no saying, "Who cares what the population of Peru is?" "We could go lift weights at Kyle's," "I mean, I guess you can come too, though I was sort of thinking maybe this time just me and Chris would go," "That's pretty good—for you, I mean," "It's not like you ever told me you like ice cream or anything," "So what if it was me who said that to her?" "I hope your brain came with a receipt," "Seriously, I didn't mean to punch you so hard there—okay, I did," "At least I'm good at lying, you can't even do that well," "You didn't say I *couldn't* show her your e-mail," "Whoop-de-do," "Get a life," and "Used to be friends—you and I used to be friends."

12:18

For some reason, Scotty Donaldson and Andrew Montego are leading me down a hallway, their arms wrapped around my back. We turn clumsily and go through a doorway. They dump me, even more clumsily, down onto a padded bench.

We're surrounded by jars filled with cotton balls, Q-tips, and bandages; posters detailing the ear, a healthy set of teeth, and perfect posture; photocopied announcements about vaccine season, a recent lice outbreak at a nearby elementary school, and the various reasons for washing your hands thirty-five times each and every day.

"Thank you, gentlemen, for helping walk Sam over here. You may go now."

I must be in Nurse Landen's office, since she's right across from me in her wrinkled skin and starched white uniform, rolling her chair in my direction.

"Nurse Landen," Andrew says, "he keeps talking about a boxing match."

"That's nice," Nurse Landen says calmly.

"Something about the square root of puberty," Andrew continues, sounding pretty confused.

"And he keeps mumbling all these—I don't know what they are—rules maybe," Scotty says. "'No' this, 'no' that. I think maybe Sam went crazy."

"Thank you, gentlemen, you may go now," Nurse Landen repeats politely, and waits until they leave.

"Sam, can you hear me?" she asks.

"Yes," I tell her, trying to remember what, or who, the square root of puberty is. I have no idea.

"How do we feel?" Nurse Landen speaks these four words in the time it would take me to list this week's spelling words, all twenty-five of them, in reverse alphabetical order. Nurse Landen is, give or take fifty years, the same age as Janitor Budds, meaning she received on-the-job medical training during the Revolutionary War. This may also have something to do with the fact that she is the size of a chimpanzee.

HOW SHE MEASURES UP:
NURSE LANDEN AND THE ANIMAL KINGDOM

YOU CAN'T MAKE THIS STUFF UP.

"My head is a little sore." This is more or less accurate, if "a little sore" can also mean "throbbing like crazy."

"I would imagine it is. They said you got whacked something awful. Said your eyes rolled all the way up and you twirled like a top." Nurse Landen slowly reaches a small, leathery hand toward my head. I'm covered in food, but the scent of her formaldehyde perfume still comes through loud and clear. "My, my, we've got ourselves quite a bump there, now don't we, young man?"

I quickly lift my own hand to the source of the throbbing, where I discover a Tootsie Roll–shaped bump on the top of my head. This is usually not a good thing, but then I remember: I should be getting my butt kicked. Right now. Right this very instant.

Sharing my skull with Tootsie seems a pretty small price to pay.

"Is everyone else at recess?" I ask.

Nurse Landen shakes her head very slowly from side to side. "Oh, no. Recess was canceled. You might be the one and only Viking not on cleanup duty, what with all that tomfoolery in the cafeteria. When will you children ever learn the importance of nutrition?"

FIVE MINUTES WITH

Tootsie

THE COOLEST BUMP IN TOWN!

Awesome:
ICE PACKS &
SOFT PILLOWS

Not Awesome:
COMBS & HATS

Dream:
SAM GETS A PADDED
HELMET FOR HIS
14th BIRTHDAY

Bet You Didn't Know:
THE LADIES CALL HIM
"MR. LIPSTICK."

Quote to Live By:
"ALWAYS FOLLOW YOUR
HEART. AND DON'T
EVER TOUCH ME."

Recess was canceled! One more reason to like food fights.

"Principal Benson attempted to telephone your mother and father but was unable to locate either of them." In the time it takes her to speak these last few sentences, I have nearly made a complete recovery. "Would you happen to have any additional telephone numbers for them? Perhaps a cellular telephone number, for instance. Unfortunately, our secretaries have only work and home telephone numbers for your mother and father in our records."

I sit up with great effort. "Why are you calling them?"

Nurse Landen smiles the kind of smile she probably used to smile back in 1794 when her mischievous sons, Floyd and Clyde, wanted to play horseshoes instead of milking the cows. "Why, so they can take you home."

"Oh." I consider this while touching Tootsie.

So I could end all this with a single phone call. Get picked up. Hide at home. Apply for Canadian citizenship, move to Toronto, live among a more peaceful people.

But I'd only be postponing the inevitable, because I

read somewhere that getting Canadian citizenship is actually pretty hard. Darn peaceful Canadians. Unless there's a serious spring snowstorm or the sudden outbreak of an airborne virus, I'll be back here at exactly this time tomorrow. The blacktop, also known as the Wagner Middle School Butt-Kicking Arena, will still be standing. And Morgan Sturtz will still want to kick mine.

"My dad's impossible to get ahold of when he's at work," I inform Nurse Landen, trying to sound disappointed. He actually works at home most of the time, in his crazy studio. He's a music engineer, which in his case means he puts together the music and sound effects that they play at football and basketball games. One time he composed this awesome introduction for Morgan and me, like we were about to play for the championship of something. I was "Your Captain!" and had played at Michigan State, which Morgan said was the best place to have played. My dad turned down the lights, and the music was so loud, I forgot I stink at sports. Instead, I felt like I was about to save the planet. We made my dad play it eleven times, until my hand hurt from high-fiving Morgan. My dad was ready for us to leave by then anyway.

"And," I continue, "my mom is in Switzerland on a business trip." If I'm going to lie, I might as well get my money's worth. My mom really is away, but only in St. Louis. She went down there to be the photographer at the wedding of some cousin of some friend of hers from college, and so she decided to stay until today to hang out with her friend.

She always used to take a lot of pictures, but then, about four years ago, the guy who was supposed to take pictures at my uncle's huge fiftieth birthday got sick at the last minute, so she filled in. Turned out she's really good at it, so she decided to start her own business.

I remember how she sat down on the edge of my bed one Sunday night and asked, "Sammy, what would you think if I went back to work?"

"What kind of work?" I asked her.

"Well"—she seemed very excited by my question because her face suddenly lit up—"how does 'Rebecca Lewis Photography' sound to you?"

And then I felt how I had like a hundred questions I wanted to ask her all at the same time, but that most of them maybe weren't so nice. Questions like: *What about me?* and *How much are you going to be gone?* and *Photography is stupid.* I guess some of them weren't really questions. But I could tell she wanted me to be happy for her, so I just said, "It sounds good." Her face stayed lit up, and she did this thing she used to do a lot but doesn't really do much anymore, where she kisses the top of my head and then breathes in very loudly before getting up and turning off the light. It took me a long time to fall asleep that night.

At first she just did everything out of our basement, but then she got her own studio, which has some pretty cool computers in it, but still, she's there way too much.

In fact, the only really good thing about her being so crazy about cameras is that we have a picture of just about every fun thing I've ever done in my entire life. Learning how to ride a bike, making chocolate-chip pancakes, jumping on my neighbor's trampoline, standing in front of Niagara Falls, you name it. Plus, a couple times she made me these pretty amazing photo albums for my birthday presents. They actually look like real books. When I turned eleven, she made me one that was just pictures from this time my parents took Morgan and me to Cedar Point, which is probably the best amusement park in the whole world.

There's this one picture in it, from right after we got off Shoot the Rapids. Both of us are totally soaked and have our hair in Mohawks. We were totally cracking up, too, because right before she took the picture, Morgan said something like, "Man, I just had to go so bad, I couldn't hold it in." So I said, "I'm so stupid! I know I should have gone before we got on." And we kept making jokes like that until after we were already dry, until my dad finally told us to knock it off.

My mom gave that picture a whole page. That used to be the best picture ever.

I looked at it this morning, because I woke up early and couldn't fall back asleep. Then I went downstairs. My dad was sitting at the kitchen table, drinking coffee and reading the newspaper. "Hey, good morning," he said. I didn't say anything, just opened the cupboard and took out the

Rice Krispies. Then he said, "You're up pretty early."

I went to the fridge, took out the milk, and finally said, "So?"

I could hear him watching me while I got a bowl and a spoon. "Everything okay, bud?" he asked.

Now he wants to know. Now, a year and a half after letting Chris into our house. Now, after not caring that I was going over to that kid's stupid house all the time (where there never were any adults) for the last year so people could drop bowling balls on my head. Now, after Morgan laughed at me in front of the whole school. I just stared at the back of the Rice Krispies box and said, like I didn't feel like talking, "Everything's just great, Dad." He didn't say much after that.

So I tell Nurse Landen, "You won't be able to get either of them right now."

"I see." She scoots to the front of her chair and lowers a foot to the floor to roll herself back to her desk. "Well, Samuel, you are welcome to remain here to recuperate as long as you would like."

Another chance to hide. But what's the point? "Actually, I think I'm okay."

"As long as you are certain." Nurse Landen hands me my gym uniform: blue shorts and a yellow T-shirt boasting, what else, the likeness of a supertough Viking.

"What's this for?" I ask her, even though I have a hunch I won't like the answer.

There's that smile again. "Well, we can't very well receive a proper education covered from head to toe in our school-mates' lunches, now can we? You may change right here. I will step out for a moment to inform Prinicipal Benson of your status and your decision."

12:21

I'm retying my shoes, trying to figure out why apple-
sauce is only partially absorbed by my laces, when a knock
comes at the door.

"Yes?"

The door springs open, a voice already speaking, "Kay,
sorry, me again." A head appears, that of Ms. Zuckerman,
the art teacher. "You wouldn't happen to have any more of
those—" The head turns, she sees me and realizes that I'm
not Nurse Landen.

I wave, don't ask why. "Hi, Ms. Zuckerman."

She steps all the way inside, giving me a view of her long, dark, frizzy hair, today's flowing scarf (blue and green, paisley pattern), a pair of orange glasses hanging from a thin purple cord around her neck, some sort of maroon silky pants-dress thing covering her legs, and, of course, her leather boots, which would look good on a pirate who drives a motorcycle on weekends.

"It's Mika, Sam." She closes her right eye, like reminding me of this has given her a headache. "Ms. Z, if you can't deal with first names."

"Sorry." I wipe my hands on the bench, trying to remove the applesauce.

"Hey, what's up? What are you doing here? Where's Nurse Landen? And what's with the getup? Don't tell me we've got another dodgeball casualty on our hands."

Allow me to state clearly that Ms. Zuckerman is not your average Wagner Middle School faculty member. Most teachers here think their job is to train us to behave like good little doggies, doggies who can also barf back facts the teachers don't even care about. But not Ms. Zuckerman, or Mika, or Ms. Z. She just tells us stuff like, "I can't teach you much about art that you don't already know. Because art's already in you. You just need to let yourself remember. We're all artists, every last one of us." She treats us like actual adults, or at least actual short adults.

"You didn't hear?" I ask, confused.

Ms. Z looks out the door, around the office, trying to figure out something that I doubt has anything to do with our conversation. "Hear what?"

How can she be this clueless? "Weren't you in the cafeteria? They called all the teachers there. Code 9–18 or something."

"9–18? No," she replies, her eyes drifting over to Nurse Landen's desk. "I meditate during lunch, so my intercom was off. Also, I don't enter the cafeteria."

This is the other thing about Ms. Z. On the one hand, she's a pretty cool person, and I usually avoid that word. Even though I stink at drawing, she actually got me to want to try it again. She gave me a book on something called "Impressionism," which I read instead of doing papier-mâché, because there's something really, really wrong about that goop. When we talked about the book later, I could tell she felt about that guy Monet the way I felt about the scientific calculator I got for my twelfth birthday. But then, on the other hand, she kind of seems like a mess most of the time. Still, she's probably my second-favorite teacher at Wagner Middle School.

"Massive food fight." I pack my clothes into the plastic bag that was holding my PE uniform. "Someone nailed me with a salad bowl."

"Where?" This gets her attention.

"Right here." And I stand up to show her Tootsie.

Ms. Z takes her hand, half covered in green paint, and puts it on my head. Somehow this makes me feel much better. "Holy crap, Sam." Yes, that's yet another way Ms. Z stands apart from her colleagues. "Morgan didn't do that to you, did he?"

"Morgan?" I pretend I have no idea what she's talking about. "Why would Morgan hit me with a salad bowl?"

Ms. Z removes her hand, crosses her arms, and says

nothing. She's half smiling and rolling her eyes, an expression that could mean any or all of the following:

- You're really smart, don't act stupid.
- Please don't try to fool me like you would, understandably, most of my coworkers. I deserve better than that, and you know it.
- I'm Mika Zuckerman, I know everything that goes on here at Wagner Middle School, so let's not pretend I don't know what I'm talking about.

Because that's the last thing about Ms. Z: She *does* know just about everything that goes on here (except massive food fights, I guess). I don't think this is part of some master plan on her part (if only because I doubt Ms. Z is the kind of person who thinks up master plans). It's just that you act differently in her room. Plus, you're allowed to talk— encouraged, even. Plus, you just sit there painting mangoes or sculpting shoes out of clay, listening to a CD of some guy playing the sitar, chatting the whole time. Meanwhile, Ms. Z walks around, checks in on how everyone's doing, tells you she thinks your project is great (and seems to really mean it), makes a couple suggestions, but then doesn't hurry off. Instead, she'll sit down, maybe work on something of her own, until, next thing you know, you're treating her like just another seventh grader. And this is even before getting to all those girls who stick around after class or show up early to talk with her about private things they won't even tell their friends. Ms. Z's room is a magnet for all gossip at Wagner Middle School.

I sit back down on the sticky bench. "It came from his table. But I don't think it was him."

"So it is true." Ms. Z plops down in Nurse Landen's chair. "You two really were going to fight at recess today."

"Yeah, it's true." No point in pretending.

"That's crazy, Sam." Ms. Z opens up one of Nurse Landen's cabinets and begins casually looking through it. "You two need to talk. You need to sort this out." She removes a small plastic container, reads the label, puts it back. "Nonviolent conflict resolution, you know?"

"DUDE, DON'T BE AN ANTI-DUDE
WITH THE ATTITUDE."

"CLOSE YOUR EYES. SHH...
LISTEN CLOSELY..
CAN YOU HEAR THAT?
THAT'S THE SOUND OF...
YOU FEELING IT!"

"IT'S OKAY. EVEN PICASSO
BLEW IT EVERY ONCE IN A WHILE."

"YOU KNOW WHY I'M SMILING?
BECAUSE IN TEN YEARS I
GET TO SAY YOU WERE IN
MY ART CLASS!"

"YES, YES, YES!!!"

MR. Z-ISMS

"Yeah, try telling that to Morgan," I say, wishing I could ask her to lead the negotiations between us.

"So, you need to apologize to him." Ms. Z removes a glass vial, unscrews the top, smells it, and shudders a bit.

I cross my arms, even if she can't see me. "Why do *I* need to apologize?"

Ms. Z momentarily stops her pillaging to offer me another version of that look. "Sam. Please. I don't think I'm exactly going out on a limb here when I say that if you two are going to fight, it probably wasn't your idea. Correct?"

"Correct." Arms still crossed.

"And you and Morgan used to be tight as thieves. Simpatico. Best buds." She bends forward and rests her forearms on her thighs. "You follow?"

"Yeah." Arms still crossed.

"And"—she takes the end of her scarf in one hand and runs the tassels along the palm of her other hand—"considering he's a jock and all, Morgan's still a decent kid, am I right?"

"Yeah, pretty much." Arms uncrossed. "Used to be, anyway."

"So"—she keeps playing with her scarf but has switched hands—"he must be extremely PO-ed about something you did."

I look down at my feet for a moment before answering. "Well, I did do this one thing."

"One thing?" I think she laughs. "Really? You did just one thing? Only one?"

Now I am mad. "What is that supposed to mean?"

"Sam, tell me something." Ms. Z is now using her scarf to clean her glasses. "What'd you get on your last report card?"

What does this have to do with anything? "A's."

She doesn't look up. "All A's?"

"Except for two A pluses. So?"

"And . . ." She breathes out onto her glasses, then goes back to cleaning them. "And Morgan, how'd he do?"

I shrug my shoulders. "How am I supposed to know? I don't remember."

"Really?" She lifts her head up and smiles at me. "You know what the capital of Tajikistan is, you know how many electrons are in a uranium atom, but you can't remember what your best friend—"

"*Ex*–best friend," I correct her.

"And"—Ms. Z holds up her glasses about six inches from her face and squints—"you expect me to believe you don't remember what Morgan got on his report card."

"Fine." I kick the bench with the back of my shoe. "He got an A, two B's, and four C's."

"A in PE?" she asks.

"Yeah, so?" I say, annoyed. "What does this have to do with anything?"

Ms. Z finally stops playing around with her glasses, sits up, and looks right at me. "Oh, I don't know. But I'd guess that he knows what you got and that he knows that you know what he got and that maybe you couldn't help being very happy about what you got whenever he saw your grades and you saw his. That, you know, you sort of spiked, just like a football, right in front of him."

The back of my neck is getting very warm, and I think Tootsie is swelling. "I didn't spike anything."

Ms. Z puts up her hands, like I need calming down. "Forget it, never mind. You're miffed about your head, I get it. So tell me, what was the one thing you *did* do?"

And I really was going to tell her—I wanted to, even—but there's Nurse Landen bursting in like it's her office, a pleasant smile quickly forced onto her face. "Why, hello, Mika. How are you feeling today?"

Ms. Z shakes her head. "Don't ask."

And then they both look at me, so I stand up and tuck my shirt into my oversized shorts. I'm about to tell Ms. Z that I'll see her soon for sixth period, but Nurse Landen speaks first.

"Samuel," she says very, very softly. "Principal Benson is waiting for you in his office."

12:25

If I weren't wearing my PE uniform so far from the

gym, if I weren't holding a plastic bag filled with my food-covered clothing, if a number of different condiments didn't squirt out of my shoes with each step, if Tootsie didn't pulse each time one of my feet hit the floor, I'd still feel extra strange, because here I am, walking the halls between the mysterious back offices deep inside Wagner Middle School.

I am walking on (and probably staining) actual carpeting.

Not particularly nice carpeting, but still, it's carpeting, which, when you compare it to the rest of the school's tiling, makes this little wing feel kind of fancy. I almost expect to see a bellboy appear from around the corner pushing a brass cart stacked high with luggage. Next (and I stop between squishy steps to make sure I'm right), the sound level in this hallway is, that's right, *quiet* (a word you only ever hear around these parts when a teacher screams, "I said, QUIET!!"). I am alone, walking through an actual student-free zone.

But none of this is one tenth as amazing as what I suddenly realize stands less than a foot from my very own hand: a doorknob connected to a door connected to a bathroom containing one, and only one, toilet.

I step inside, and yes, almost too good to be true, the door has something called a "lock" on it, giving me access to something called "privacy."

I try to look at myself in the mirror, only it's hung at adult height. Thankfully, there's a tall wooden block under the sink (I should remember to thank Nurse Landen for that), so I grab it and hop on up. Turns out that the lunchtime glop in my hair works like styling gel. My Vikings shirt is size XS, but it's still too big in the shoulders. I should send Santa a note asking for shoulders this year.

Which reminds me of something: passing notes. If you're wondering if I have a rule about passing notes, I do. It's pretty complicated, so pay attention.

DON'T EVER PASS NOTES. DON'T EVEN WRITE THEM. JUST DON'T. EVER. EVER!

Let's go back to last Friday. Mr. Griegs's class. Mr. Griegs was trying to take us back to 1758, to that boring social studies unit for some reason named "The French and Indian War." Class was almost over and pretty much no one was paying attention anymore, so Mr. Griegs called upon his terrifying "Point and Answer or Else" review technique. He goes back a day or two, says some random sentence from then, but leaves out the last word and points at a student, whose job it is to finish the sentence before Mr. Griegs loses patience and points at someone else. The only interesting part of the whole exercise is seeing how mad he gets if he has to point at more than two people to get a correct answer.

"In Canada the French and Indian War is known as"—arm outstretched—"Kelsey Rackowski!"

Kelsey Rackowski squirms, looks around the room like the answer might be on a wall somewhere. "Um, the battle of . . ."

Mr. Griegs bites his mustache and whips his arm to the other side of the room. "Justin Kellerman!"

Justin Kellerman holds his arms up to protect himself, forgetting he's also supposed to say something.

Steam begins coming out of Mr. Griegs's ears. He won't be able to last much longer, so it's me to the rescue.

"Sam Lewis!"

I look up from my doodling. "The Seven Years' War," I say, sparing us all from a dreaded "Three Strikes and You All Have Extra Homework" situation.

Of course, Mr. Griegs doesn't say "good" or anything like that, he just jumps to the next question. Eventually, he gets to Morgan, who gets the easiest question in the history of seventh-grade social studies, because Mr. Griegs is definitely the kind of teacher who favors jocks. "Even though it's called the French and Indian War, this war was in fact between France and"—arm outstretched—"Morgan Sturtz!"

I lean to the side to watch the back of Morgan as he tries to answer. Mr. Griegs is actually smiling at him, as if being nice could make Morgan smart again.

"Uh, France and India?"

I know brains aren't muscles, but maybe they do shrink if you don't use them, because two years ago Morgan would never have said something even a quarter that stupid. I mean, he used to be pretty great at remembering dates and stuff. Who knows what happened to him. All I do know is, at that point, I couldn't help it. I turned to a blank page in my notebook. I wrote *Morgan is so dumb* right in the middle. I quietly tore out the page and carefully folded it into a paper airplane. Ms. Z taught us how to make about fifteen different kinds of airplanes at the beginning of the year in a unit she called "The Art of Science and the Science of Art." She even told us we could write a short message down the middle, because then you could fly a message to a friend and the message would be hidden until someone unfolded it. So

for a while, before he got moved, Morgan and I would pass
each other notes this way when Mr. Griegs wasn't looking.

THE SHARK ATTACK

THE SURREALIST

THE CIRCLE
OF GLORY

THE FLYING W

THE LOOP-THE-LOOP

THE SHOW-OFF

I wasn't even planning on passing this note to anyone, I was just bored. Okay, maybe I was also a little mad at Morgan for laughing when Chris (and Jordan and Brandon) made fun of me at lunch (so what if I still use my Spider-Man Thermos sometimes?). Maybe I finally got sick of Morgan laughing at me then and at the pep rally and about twenty times in between. Anyway, all I did was finish the airplane and set it on the edge of my desk. Only about ten seconds later Drake Carter, who sits next to me, lifted up and slammed down his social studies book. He was celebrating his "Fort Ticonderoga" response, which successfully finished the sentence, "The French called this Fort Carillon, but the British called it . . ." All at once: a loud bam, a strong gust, an airplane taking off from my desk, the end-of-the-period bell, and thirty kids racing out of the classroom. I tried to find the airplane. I looked everywhere. I even got on my hands and knees. But it was gone.

After worrying about it nonstop all day Friday, I woke up Saturday realizing I had nothing to worry about. It's not like my name was on it. There's no way it flew all the way to

Morgan. Mr. Budds had probably thrown it out already.

Then on Sunday, after calling Morgan's house and having his mom say to me, for the tenth time in the last month, "Oh, hi, Sam. Morgan went out for a bike ride," I decided to go on one myself. I rode by Chris's house, not because I wanted to go inside, but just to see if Morgan's bike might be parked in front. Only, my luck, there on the driveway were Morgan, Chris, Jordan, and Brandon. Before if I could decide if going over there was a good idea or not, they saw me. Chris smiled and pumped his fist, which, unless he had finally decided he was ready for some tutoring in algebra, was not a good sign. But it was too late, I couldn't just turn around. So I biked over.

I looked at Morgan, who was not happy to see me. Everyone else was silent, but in a *Oh boy, when this silence ends, we're going to have fun!* kind of way.

"Hey, guys," I said, trying to sound normal. "What's up?"

Morgan reached into one of his pockets and pulled out a crumpled sheet of paper. Even though it was just a little ball, I knew.

I tried pretending I didn't know what it was for a few

seconds, but even if I really didn't know, Morgan's face would still have made me feel guilty. He didn't look very mad, just a little. But the rest of him looked super calm, meaning he looked mostly calm and a little mad, which told me, I could see it in his eyes, that he had already decided what was about to happen. And it wasn't going to be good.

Still, I did my best to talk like I didn't know what was happening. "What's that?" I said, pretending I couldn't see it in his expression.

"You're dead, man," Morgan answered, while the others said things like "Yeah," "Cool," and "Finally."

"What are you talking about?" I asked innocently.

He opened up the paper and walked over to me and my bike. I was holding on to the handlebars, my bike still under me. He held it up to my face. "Don't tell me that's not your writing."

I tried to smile. "That's not—"

"Now you're gonna lie about it too, man," Morgan said, shaking his head, which had started turning red.

At which point I started slowly walking my bike backward, trying to figure out how far I needed to go before I could escape.

"If you think I'm dumb, why don't you just say it to my face?" he continued, his face getting more and more red. "C'mon."

"I don't. I don't think you're dumb," I tried, but I've never been good at lying. So maybe I really do think he is dumb, or something else not so nice. Whatever, it was time to get out of there, so I pushed off and started biking away as fast as I could.

At which point Morgan screamed, still holding up the paper, "Go ahead, Sam, run away. Doesn't matter, because I am totally going to kick your butt tomorrow at recess. I'm serious!"

And that's why you shouldn't even write notes, ever.

"Samuel?" It's Nurse Landen, knocking softly on the bottom third of the door. "Samuel, are you in there?"

I pretend I'm not, because maybe I could be somewhere else, like, oh, I don't know, Australia.

"Samuel, I know you're in there. I can hear the water running. Samuel, Principal Benson is waiting for you."

So I give up, because I always give up.

12:28

Ladies and gentlemen of the jury, Nurse Landen is a liar!

Let the record show that Nurse Landen specifically said (twice!), "Principal Benson is waiting for you."

Let the record show that she did *not* say, "Principal Benson is waiting for you in his office, where you'll also find Morgan Sturtz and Chris Tripadero."

I rest my case.

Because that's a way different thing to prepare yourself for, especially when you're not you, but me. Because if I knew I'd be walking into this particular four-person get-together, I'd be hiding at the bottom of a trash can in a nearby bathroom right now, trying to figure out how to live off whatever nutrients could be wrung out of the outfit in this plastic bag. Instead, I'm standing in my PE uniform, looking at Morgan and Chris in their PE uniforms, looking at Morgan and Chris looking at me, and looking for a place to sit.

Chris's always-stomach-turning mouth has that caged-rat look to it, if this caged rat thought his cage was a fun place to hang out. Morgan's expression is a little harder to read, because he's much better than Chris at hiding whatever hides behind it. His jaw muscles are clenched, his eyebrows are lowered, and his eyes can't find a single thing to settle on. If I had to guess, I'd say he's mad (at me), scared (of Principal Benson), and confused (by being mad and scared at the same time).

"Hello, Samuel." Oh, right, Principal Benson and his deep, deep voice are also here. The other thing you should know about Principal Benson is that he has super huge

sideburns. The kind that everyone has in movies about the
Civil War. I wonder if he rides to school on a horse.

AND **HAIR** THEY ARE!
THE WAGNER MIDDLE SCHOOL
"WHY SHAVE IT ALL?"
ALL-STARS!

MR. GRIEGS
"The DEAD CATERPILLAR"

MR. MOREHEAD
"THE FACE-O-FOREST"

PRINCIPAL BENSON
"THE MUTTONCHOPS"

MR. DONNELLY
"WHERED THE REST OF IT GO?"

117

"Hi, Principal Benson." Please offer to get me a chair. Or, better yet, please invite me to go find a chair myself so that I can calm down or, more likely, run straight for the Canadian border. Please, please, please.

Principal Benson slowly looks around the room and, it appears for the first time, does the chairs-minus-people math. "I hope you don't mind standing, Samuel. We seem to be fresh out of seats."

"No, sir, that's fine." Standing might put me at some sort of physical advantage, if Morgan weren't, sitting down, my height. Not to mention me in my PE uniform versus Morgan in his, since he looks ready to star in the photo shoot for the PE uniform catalog.

Either Chris cackles or I just remember him cackling.

Principal Benson rests his hands on his massive wooden desk, his fingers interwoven for maximum "what I'm about to say to you is of great importance" effect.

He clears his throat. "Gentlemen, would one of you like to tell me what that is on the wall behind me?"

"A picture of a bunch of people parachuting?" I answer. "It says 'Teamwork' underneath."

"Well, yes." Principal Benson begins to turn around, but decides against it. "But next to that, what do you see?"

"The Viking Code, sir," Morgan says quietly.

"Correct, Morgan"—Principal Benson nods—"the Viking Code. And what is the Viking Code?"

Chris begins to make some sort of sound, and not a smart one, but magically catches himself first.

"Uh, it's a list of words that start with the letters in 'Viking,'" Morgan answers.

"Indeed, it is," Principal Benson tells us. "Indeed, it is. But that tells us only the outlines of the code, its contours." He pauses and looks at each one of us separately. "It does not tell us its contents. Which are?"

A long, awkward silence, until I ask, "Do you want us to tell you the words?"

"Yes"—long, dramatic exhale—"would you be so kind, Samuel?"

"Okay, well, 'Virtue'—"

"Yes, virtue." Principal Benson turns his head a bit. "Though *V* is not the most common letter, you might be surprised to know how many fine candidates there were that begin with *V.* 'Valor,' 'vigor,' 'victory.' I initially supported 'victory,' but Assistant Principal Hart persuaded me of, well"—Principal Benson chuckles for a second—"the virtues of 'virtue.'" After running a thumb along one of his chops, he says to himself, "I still think 'victory' would have made a fine choice." Then he moves his hand to his chin and says, "You may continue."

"'Integrity,'" I respond.

"Yes, yes, integrity," Principal Benson responds. "The easiest decision of that evening. Everyone instantly recognized 'integrity' to be a winner. Next?"

"'Knowledge.'"

"Correct. Now, here I had to take issue." Principal Benson points at Morgan. "Because the first two words, clearly, refer to qualities we would like to see in our students here at Wagner Middle School. A Viking *acts* with virtue. A Viking *acts* with"—Principal Benson closes his fist for emphasis—"integrity. But can a Viking act with knowledge? This was my question, until Carolyn Brewer, the esteemed head of our PTA, said, 'Otis, perhaps these are things our students *pursue*. A Viking *pursues* virtue, integrity, and knowledge.' We're lucky to have Carolyn on board, we truly are. Continue, gentlemen."

"'Intelligence,'" Morgan reads.

"Yes, intelligence. There was quick consensus on 'integrity,' but this second *I*, gentlemen, was a challenge. A large parent bloc advocated for 'incorruptibility,' while a number of teachers rallied around 'inquisitiveness,' but I helped everyone see the value of something a little more, how should I say, intelligible." Principal Benson chuckles, and I try to join in, but can't. "Samuel, why don't you give us the rest?"

"Okay." My legs are getting tired. "'Never give up' and 'greatness.'"

Principal Benson chuckles yet again for a second. "Now, you'd think, '*N*, there must be a million winning terms that begin with *N*.' Well, you'd be surprised. 'Niceness,' that was about all we could find, even after poring over our library's thesaurus. Made me wish I had thrown my hat in the ring for the job over at Nichols. 'Raider' would give you 'responsibility' and 'discipline.' But we carried on, and I think you'll agree with me when I say that we ended on a high note."

SAM'S
THE VIKING CODE

VERY STUPID SCHOOL.

INCREDIBLE THAT ANYONE LEARNS ANYTHING HERE.

KIDS KAN'T EVEN SPELL. (PLUS THEY'RE MEAN.)

I WISH I WENT TO A DIFFERENT SCHOOL.

NO, I'M NOT JOKING.

GET ME OUT OF HERE.

* (MAY REQUIRE ADULT SUPERVISION)

ACTUAL VIKING CODES ENCOURAGED VIOLENCE AND PILLAGING.

A few moments of awkward silence.

"So, gentlemen"—Principal Benson returns his hands to

their original "I'm a man of great wisdom" position—"that is the *what* of the Viking Code. But can anyone explain to us the *why* of the code?"

I turn to Morgan for a moment. He notices and nods his head at me quickly, like I better help out here.

"It is how we're supposed to behave, sir," I say.

"Exactly!" Principal Benson responds with a big smile of satisfaction, like this might explain the last three minutes. "*Who* is a Viking? *Who* should a Viking aspire to be? Virtue. Integrity. Knowledge. Intelligence. Never give up. Greatness." Principal Benson's face goes blank for a moment, and he says under his breath, "Can't believe that's all we could get for *N*." But he recovers quickly, suddenly stands up, and begins pacing behind his desk. "Now, I ask you, gentlemen, did the acts committed in our cafeteria just moments ago measure up to the Viking Code?"

"No, sir," we answer together. Or at least Morgan and I answer together.

"No, no they did not," Principal Benson reminds us. "They absolutely did not. There is no integrity in throwing applesauce. There is no greatness to be had in pelting a fellow Viking with a tater tot. And knocking out a fellow Viking with a reinforced, heavy-duty salad bowl made from eighty-percent postconsumer recycled plastics is not—I repeat, *not*—an act of intelligence. Thankfully, our very own Mr. Griegs, who was recently transported to Glen Hills General for posttraumatic counseling, spearheaded our investigation aimed at reconstructing the final moments leading up to that last, dastardly act. According to the testimony of no fewer than *three* eyewitnesses, one of these two young men"—Principal Benson points across his desk and glares accusingly at Morgan and Chris—"is responsible for your injury, Samuel."

Arm still extended, Principal Benson turns back to me. "Unfortunately, neither has yet admitted guilt. We have been waiting for you to regain consciousness with the hopes that you yourself could identify your assailant, who, you can be sure"—eyes back on Morgan and Chris—"shall pay a very stiff price for such a wanton violation of the Viking Code. A very stiff price indeed." Principal Benson pauses and crosses his arms.

I've got to admit the suspense is killing me (which would be easier to wait through if I had a chair). "*Expulsion* from Wagner Middle School and a possible criminal investigation." Principal Benson sits back down, relaces his fingers, and waits for me to pick out the guilty party.

I look over at Morgan and Chris, whose fates now rest in my sweaty hands. Chris snarls and rolls his eyes, his face a little more green than usual. I almost feel pity for him. Almost. Okay, I don't. Not at all.

But Morgan's face makes more sense. Mouth shut tight, eyes wide with shame and regret. Maybe a little guilt, too. Or more than a little bit.

12:33

Okay, so maybe by this point you doubt that Morgan
and I were really friends at all by the start of this school year.
Sure, you say, kickball in first grade. Sand castles and slush-
ies at the beach in second grade. LEGO blocks and skate-
boards in third grade. A trip to Chicago with his family in
fourth grade. SpongeBob and sleepovers in fifth grade. Fine.

But middle school? What do you guys have in common
at this point? Nothing, you say. He's popular; you're not. He
couldn't care less about studying; you like hanging out at

bookstores. He's tall enough to ride the Millennium Force roller coaster at Cedar Point; you wish booster seats were considered cool and made available in the cafeteria. Maybe you were still *friendly* in sixth grade. Maybe you were the final kid added to his birthday list last year (someone else canceled and the bowling alley needed at least ten). Maybe you got assigned to do a science project together this year, which got you one final Sunday afternoon at his house. Maybe he's been that kind of friend lately. But a *best* friend? Sam Lewis, you say, c'mon, who are you kidding?

Well, to all you doubters out there, I have a short and simple (and totally awesome) answer:

Alien Wars.

If you know what Alien Wars is, you may skip to the next paragraph, and feel free to devote the time you save by not reading the following sentences to appreciate Alien Wars once again. If you are not familiar with Alien Wars, find the nearest chalkboard and write on it one hundred times, *I promise to get Alien Wars right away and play it all the time.* Wait, no, forget that, you've already waited long enough. Skip the chalkboard part and just go get it already. And then play. All the time. Until your thumb hurts. Then take a three-minute break. Then continue playing. Then play through the pain, it's worth it, trust me. I'd remind you to scream with joy, *Alien Wars is the best game ever!* but I'm pretty sure you won't have much trouble remembering that one.

All right, so, how can I put this? Alien Wars is the very most extremely bestest awesomest "first-person shooter game" of all time, which means that what you see on the screen is what your player sees. And, and, *and,* your player just so happens to hold a too-awesome-to-believe weapon, your player who has no choice but to shoot pretty much everything that shows up on the screen. Because it's the twenty-fourth century and you're Viko Paz, a half-man, half-alien supersoldier, defending the Interstellar Alliance against the dreaded Galactic Federation (curses to you, Galactic Federation!). Okay, I am doing my best right now to resist spending the next seven hours explaining the entire game to you. So let's just put it this way: If you like pretending to shoot things, if you like pretending to be the baddest shooter in the twenty-fourth century, if you like your shoot-

ing to be part of an actual story, in this case a military campaign to save the universe, then Alien Wars = ten times more
fun than winning the Novi Invitational.

"TOOLS of THE TRADE" -OR- "FRIENDS YOU'LL MAKE PLAYING ALIEN WARS"

PEW
PEW
PEW!

ALPHA FUSION BLASTER
DON'T POINT AT THINGS YOU LIKE.

GAMMA GRENADE LAUNCHER
THE SECRET TO CROWD CONTROL

BETA FUSION BLASTER
ONE SHOT IS ALL IT TAKES.

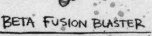

OMEGA SMART BOMB

IF IT'S ON THE SCREEN,
SOON IT WON'T BE.

DELTA AIR SAW ✳
BECAUSE SOMETIMES YOU WANT
TO CUT 'EM IN HALF.

✳ CAUTION:
SHARP EDGES

And, oh yeah, Alien Wars allows multiplayer campaigns, meaning that two people (such as MorSam) can play together.

Saturday morning, February, last year. My mom is going to be at her studio all day. Morgan is spending the weekend at our place, because his parents are in Boston visiting his older brother at college. The night before, we talked about bowling or a movie or a trip to Twelve Oaks Mall. But that morning my dad comes into my room, where Morgan and I are still half sleeping.

"Hey, guys," he says, "anyone want to guess how cold it is outside right now?"

I look out the window, like I might be able to tell by examining the shade of gray everywhere. Then I look at Morgan, who says, "I don't know, five?"

"Five would be balmy, Morgan," my dad answers. "Five would be trip-to-the-beach weather."

"Five *below*," I say.

"Getting there," my dad says. "How does four*teen* below sound? And that's without the windchill. So, um, sorry, guys, but you'll have to come up with an indoor plan. We're not going anywhere. I've got a major deadline anyway." And then he turns around and leaves the room.

We look at each other for a few moments. "Hey, Lew," Morgan says. "Pay you five bucks to go outside in your underwear."

"I'll pay you ten bucks to go outside in mine." I smile.

"Nasty! No way." He gets up and drags me by the foot out of my bed. "What are we going to do all day?"

I think for a bit, then start nodding my head. "Alien. Wars. Marathon!"

This particular Saturday in February will forever be known as The Absolutely Most Amazing Day Ever (TAMADE). On TAMADE, Morgan and I became the greatest Alien Wars team in the history of great Alien Wars teams.

Morgan starred as Viko Paz. I costarred as Kedi Balagan.

Our matching skills—my knowledge of landscapes, weaponry, and our adversaries (not to mention timing with smart bombs), Morgan's finger strength, eye-hand coordination, and extremely large vocabulary when it comes to yelling things at our enemies (things I definitely *can't* repeat here)—made us the perfect team. I navigated and provided backup, allowing Morgan to focus his energies on killing anyone who messed with us.

And a lot of unfortunate creatures messed with us.

We saved the universe that day.

At approximately 7:30 p.m. that Saturday (yes, that would be nine hours later—nine hours, three pizzas, two bags of Cheetos, and four liters of Mr. Pibb later, to be exact), Viko Paz and Kedi Balagan reached the final battle on the desert planet, Pulzar.

"Lock and load, Paz, this is it!" I said.

"See you on the other side, Kedi!" Morgan answered.

The drums were going nuts in the background, until my dad came out to see what all the noise was about. He stood there opposite the nine-million-inch big-screen TV we got for Christmas and witnessed the whole thing. Our thumbs were about to fall off, but somehow we killed the last guy who needed killing.

Then things got real, real quiet.

Suddenly, the mother ship appeared and beamed us up.

The screen turned black, and we just sat there in silence together, until Morgan said, "Wow."

Then I said, "Wow."

Then Morgan said, "Wow," again.

I stood up and screamed, "Yes!"

Morgan did the same. We shared the best high five in high-fiving history. We ran around the room. We hugged my dad. We hugged the TV. We kissed the Alien Wars case. We each took an empty two-liter bottle of Mr. Pibb and started bashing each other over the head in celebration, screaming, "YE-E-E-E-E-SSSSSSS!!!!!" the whole time.

And then we were silent, because sometimes words just ruin things.

Right then I felt every bit as good as I felt when I found out I scored in the ninety-seventh percentile on the PSAT as a sixth grader (which is this huge test you're not even supposed to take until tenth grade). I felt like the king of the universe on TAMADE, I really did. Actually, I felt even better on TAMADE than I did after conquering the PSAT. I felt like one of two kings, like a king who wouldn't be a king without the other king.

We were the perfect team on TAMADE. No one bothered us, no one pitted one of us against the other, and no one cared one bit about what he couldn't do. Morgan didn't care that he never knew exactly where we were in the galaxy, because he knew I knew. And I didn't care that I have this annoying habit of pressing the X button instead of the Y, because I knew Morgan would clean up my mistakes. We played together, we won together.

But we don't play together anymore.

Don't get me wrong, scoring in the ninety-seventh percentile on the PSAT as a sixth grader is a pretty big deal, since it means I might be smarter than ninety-seven out of one hundred *sixteen*-year-olds. Great, now you probably think I'm bragging again too. So, okay, first thing, I don't exactly mean smarter, or not just smarter. Because, well, I actually study this stuff, a lot. I mean, it's not like anyone is born knowing geometry. Look, I like math. There, I admit it. I, Sam Lewis, like math. Heck, I love it. I love the numbers and the rules and the way an equation looks once you've worked it all out and double-checked that everything's right. Which is one more thing I can't really tell anyone. It seems like everyone at this stupid school thinks I'm either a loser nerd or a conceited brainiac or a lucky freak.

The only people (other than Mr. Glassner and the ArithmeWeirdos) I could tell about the PSAT were my parents, and they didn't act that surprised, even if they did take me out for ice cream to celebrate. The problem with my parents is they both have this funny way of thinking that my scores and my grades are the only things they really need to know about me. Like a few months ago when we got report cards. We always get them on a half-day Friday at school. I found out that Morgan, Chris, and Brandon were going to the mall in the afternoon without me. So I go straight home with my stupid report card. When my parents see it, they just keep telling me I'm perfect. They can't even tell anything is wrong, because they don't think anything else could matter. Like all A's makes you perfect. But what's so perfect about being a midget with no friends who gets straight A's?

Plus, Morgan doesn't even care about my grades, or my scores. Lately, whenever he finds out about me acing a test or something, he just gives me that face of his, the one where half his mouth curls up and his eyes get a little bigger than normal and he looks like he's getting kind of sick. Sick of me.

Which is exactly the opposite of how he looked at me after winning Alien Wars. I know, I just know, that Morgan felt exactly the same as me then, because when Viko said, "Kedi, where would I be without you?" every fifteen minutes for nine hours, he had to mean it, at least a little.

So maybe Morgan threw the bowl or maybe he didn't. I have no idea. All I know is getting him kicked out of school isn't going to get us to TAMADE II. And looking at him here in the principal's office, with him looking at me, him knowing that his expulsion might be just a word away, I swear I can see him trying to apologize without saying anything, because it's true what Ms. Z said, he *is* a decent kid. Maybe he wishes we could get back together and be friends again before the next Greatest Video Game Ever comes out—maybe he actually wants nothing more than another day below that massive TV. Maybe he knows that TAMADE almost made all the other differences between us not matter, and maybe he still believes that TAMADE II will do that again. But that can't exactly happen if he has to enroll at St. Theobald.

As for Chris, I'd love to get him out of this school and out of my life, but I don't trust the guy. I don't want to be the kid he thinks about all day while serving time at the Park County Home for Screwups, the kid he thinks about getting revenge on for sending him there in the first place. I might be a coward (okay, I am a coward, I'm definitely a coward), but I'm not a stupid coward.

Plus, honestly, I really have no idea who threw the thing.

"Principal Benson." I'm staring at the floor.

"Yes, Samuel."

I shrug my shoulders, look right at Morgan, and fight off the urge to smile. "I didn't see who did it. There was too much other stuff going on."

Morgan's head pokes forward, like he can't believe what he just heard.

"Are you certain?" Principal Benson may be threatening me, but I don't care.

"Yes."

Principal Benson leans across his desk toward Morgan and Chris. "Absolutely certain?"

"Yes, sir." I nod. "I am."

"Very well," Principal Benson says quickly. "Thank you for your time and cooperation, Samuel. You may go to your next class. Sixth period is about to begin. Mr. Sturtz and Mr. Tripadero will remain here, as I am not yet through with them."

12:39

"Hey, Sam!" Dave Benedicts screams, and heads
my way.

"Sam's here!" Emily Garlocki yells, and starts running
in my direction.

"Sam! You guys, it's Sam!" Candace Gonzalez announces
as she sprints toward me, waving her arms for everyone to
follow.

I'm standing in the main hallway between the lockers
and the front entrance to the school. Voices and Vikings

140

come at me from every direction: from every row of lockers, from the science hallway, from the gym, from the cafeteria. Everywhere I look, Vikings in their PE uniforms. Vikings looking at me with disbelief, like I was just released from a prisoner of war camp. The yellow-and-blue circle surrounding me starts asking questions.

Max Neuman: "Didn't you go to the hospital?"

Tracey Blocker: "How'd they clean up all that blood so fast?"

Chase Abbot: "Are Chris and Morgan still in there?"

Megan Zakovitch: "Did you get them kicked out?"

Vijay Reedy: "Why don't you have brain damage?"

Vijay appears disappointed and so has been disqualified from the "Who Will Replace Morgan as Sam's Best Friend, If It Comes to That" competition. Not that his chances were great to begin with.

I try to answer everyone, but they just won't shut up. Some of them are pushing closer, some of them are holding their arms out, preventing the ones pushing closer from getting closer, because, I suddenly realize:

I'm a celebrity!

Not only was I supposed to be done getting my butt kicked right around now, not only was I instead knocked out during the food fight, not only did the gossip machine have everyone convinced I was in a coma, not only did I just walk out, all by myself and under my own power, from the Wagner Middle School back offices, not only might I have valuable information about the fate of Chris and Morgan, but I—because of that whole butt kicking/getting knocked out/ falling into a coma/being in the offices thing—I may have just *decided* their fates.

"Let him talk! Let him talk!" These are the words of Jess Miller, captain of the football team, student council president, and the guy keeping the most-popular-kid-at-school chair warm for Morgan.

It's too bad that Principal Benson's effort to install surveillance cameras throughout Wagner Middle School failed, because if there were cameras, I could, after school today (if I'm still alive by then), do something risky and brilliant in order to get a video copy of me in the middle of this giant circle of students.

THE WAGNER MIDDLE SCHOOL
HOW-TO HANDBOOK, PG. 47:

THIS COULD BE YOU!

"HOW to MAKE A CIRCLE OF STUDENTS
IN 30 SECONDS OR LESS."

Step 1: WAIT UNTIL IT'S IN BETWEEN PERIODS.

Step 2: GO INTO ONE OF THE MAIN HALLWAYS.

Step 3: SCREAM LOUDLY, LIKE YOU'RE IN HORRIBLE PAIN -OR- START A FIGHT -OR- GET AN ANGRY TEACHER TO YELL AT YOU -OR- APPEAR SUDDENLY AFTER EVERYONE THOUGHT YOU WERE GONE FOREVER -OR- THROW UP -OR- SLIP AND FALL[1] -OR- BEND OVER AND RIP YOUR PANTS.[2]

!!!!

1) SLIPPING & FALLING ON THROW-UP EQUALS EXTRA-LARGE CIRCLE.

2) EXPOSED UNDERWEAR EQUALS EVEN BIGGER CIRCLE THAN SLIPPING AND FALLING ON PUKE.

STEP 4: COUNT TO TEN. ENJOY!

✱ NOTE: DO NOT CREATE A CIRCLE IF IT'S IMPORTANT TO GET TO YOUR NEXT CLASS ON TIME.

Extremely cool and sometimes frightening eighth graders like Brett Cousins, Stu Jurvacious, and Jenny Kimmel (yes, girls can be frightening) are hoping *I'll* talk to them, are trying to get closer to *me* because I know something they don't, because *I'm* someone they're not.

Now I understand why some kids do really bad things, because I might just be willing to get into a fight every Monday (but with someone a lot smaller than Morgan) if it would make this circle thing more common.

I raise my hand, attempting to quiet the crowd but not really minding the noise, because I don't have any idea what I'll say after I tell them I'm fine. *I decided maybe Morgan will still like me if I let him off, and I'm too scared of Chris to get him in trouble,* probably would not be the best way to keep my new cool-guy status.

Instead, I just say, "Please, please—"

But before I'm even done with my second "please, please" I hear the crowd behind me get extra loud. I turn around and see half my circle running down the hall in the direction I just came from, followed (if all the people flying past me right now are any clue) by the other half of what was my circle of coolness.

I run after the crowd, even though there's no real point. I won't be able to see a thing from the edge of the new circle forming at the other end of the hall anyway. My run turns into a jog and then a walk, and then I pretty much stop when I hear a familiar voice:

"Sam, hey, wait up." It's Amy, who was probably stuck at the far edge of my circle. She's wearing her PE uniform, a sliver of blue shorts sticking out from under her oversized XS T-shirt.

"Hey, Amy." I nod my head a bit, as if I'm still cool.

"Are you okay?" Amy searches for any obvious injuries.

"Yeah, I'm fine." I listen to the new source of noise, missing my fame. "Just a little bump on my head."

"Where?" Amy asks.

I look back at Amy, who waits for my answer. "I just told you, on my head."

"No, silly." Amy rolls her eyes. "*Where* on your head?"

"Oh." So I lower my head a bit and carefully touch Tootsie with my fingers.

Then I feel another set of fingers touch mine. I lift my eyes to see Amy's small arm.

"Oh my God, Sam." She sounds horrified. "That's huge."

"I know." And then I don't say anything else, because all of a sudden I can't talk.

"Does it hurt?" she asks, hand still on my head.

I think the rest of me might be melting.

After, like, ten seconds I somehow get my mouth to say, "Nah, not really," very slowly, which sort of sounds cool that way.

"Not really?!" She's not buying it.

"It kills." I may be giggling.

"I'm sorry, Sam." And I can tell she actually is. "I'm really sorry."

Then neither of us says a thing. I'm pretty sure I can hear our silence loud and clear in the middle of the roar coming from the other end of the hallway, because Amy just keeps her hand on the top of my head. Even though the pressure of her tiny fingers hurts, it feels good, too. Feels good more than it hurts. Too bad I didn't get creamed by

146

two bowls, because Amy happens to have two hands.

The floor starts to shake, and me and Amy turn to see Mr. Rozier and Ms. Ruyak, the two largest teachers at school, angrily heading toward us.

"Break it up!" he yells.

Oh man, busted for PDA (public display of affection). Great. I unmelt super fast, pull my head back, and start trying to remember if there are any good hiding places nearby.

"Off to class! Now!" she adds.

Amy, looking off to the side like I'm not even there, has quickly glued her arms to her sides. The two giant teachers blow right past us at full speed, and I'm pretty sure Amy's hair flies up in the air as they rush by. They get to the new circle at the end of the hall and start flinging bodies out of the way and threatening anyone who doesn't disappear immediately. Most everyone is gone in a matter of seconds, letting us see who was at the center of that circle: Morgan and Chris.

Just then the bell rings. I'd worry about being late, but when everyone's tardy, no one is.

"Uh," Amy says, pulling on the bottom of her shorts and still not looking at me, "I better go get my clarinet. Mr. Garfine gets pretty miffed when we're late for band."

"Yeah." I fix my hair and try to figure out why my tongue feels like it's been replaced by a rubber surfboard. "I probably should get to art. I need to put the glaze on my isosceles triangle before Ms. Z puts it back in the kiln."

Amy laughs and walks off down the hall. I turn in the other direction and see Morgan and Chris being escorted by Mr. Rozier, because they have him for science this period. Just before they turn a corner, Chris notices me. He points at me and then at Morgan. Then he nods his head and smiles like everything is A-OK.

Which means that nothing is.

12:46

It takes a couple minutes for everyone to calm down, but after saying "Okay, people" about eleven times, Ms. Z finally has our attention. She holds her hands in front of her chest in a prayer position. "Okay, gang, here's the deal. Some major you-know-what just went down in the cafeteria. Some of you probably dug it, but some of you could probably, you know, use some therapy to work through the kind of stuff that a person might have to work through after surviving a food fight. So that's what we're going to do today. Make some art to work through it, or just—"

"Can we have another food fight instead?" Tim Mesinbrink shouts.

"No, Tim." Ms. Z smiles and sighs. "I'm sorry to inform you we cannot. But this is what you can do: You can draw a picture of the food fight or a food fight you'd like to have. Or paint a picture about either. Or take some clay and sculpt, you know, the likeness of all the food that wound up down your pants." Everyone laughs. "You can even do something a little abstract. When you close your eyes and think about the food fight, what colors do you see? What shapes? Make those. Okay? Cool. One more thing. We're going to try something called 'flash art.' To get at that gut feeling. You don't want to overthink the creative impulse. So five minutes. Then we'll share—workshop our pieces."

The class jumps right in. A couple minutes later, after some very loud laughter from his corner of the room, Drake Carter says, "Ms. Z, I'm ready."

Ms. Z screams from behind a giant closet in the corner: "Wow, Drake, you really put the 'flash' back in flash art."

150

Then she peeks her head out. "You sure you don't want to put any finishing touches on it?"

"Nah, Ms. Z," Drake says, giggling, "I don't think I really want to touch it at all."

A minute later Drake is standing in front of the class with a half-crumpled piece of paper, which is mostly white, except for something yellowish and maybe a little green in the middle. Ms. Z is looking at it confused. "Is that paint, Drake, or did you do something multimedia here?"

"It's"—Drake's shoulders shake as he tries to stop laughing—"it's some of the Twinkie I put up Fernando's nose!"

Ms. Z almost starts talking about three different times until she finally asks, taking a step away from the paper, "So, that's a painting of the Twinkie, or just—"

"No! It's the Twinkie! He blew his nose on this!"

Everyone in class says either "Ugh," "Yuck," or "Gross," but in a "Drake is awesome" kind of way.

Meanwhile, I can barely focus, since I can think of only one thing: What happened to Morgan and Chris? And what was Chris smiling about? Okay, two things.

151

I turn to Sage Paley, who's got a bunch of pastels in front of her. "Sage."

Lost in her art, she doesn't respond, so I try again. "Sage." She looks up at me confused, like she's only learning just now that I've been sitting next to her in this class for the last eight months. Instead of actually saying anything, she tucks some of her long, wavy brown hair behind one of her ears. "Sage, do you know what happened to Morgan and Chris?"

Sage blinks her big, spacey eyes a few times. "Sam," she finally says, speaking my name slowly, half question, half statement.

"What? What?" I ask, anxious for any news she may have.

She points at her drawing. "Does that look like gluten-free pasta to you?"

I turn in the other direction and softly tap Doug McDougal's shoulder. He sits slouched over something I can't see.

"Doug. Hey, Doug. Doug." Because Doug McDougal doesn't just have "Doug" in both his first and his last name, he's the kind of kid you need to call a few times if you expect him to notice.

"Huh?" he says without moving.

I lower my head down to our table, trying to get Doug's attention. "Doug, do you know what happened with Morgan and Chris?"

Doug sits up just enough to turn his rock of a head in my direction, allowing me a clear view of his beat-up spiral notebook. Instead of answering my question, he just stares at me, an idiotic smile across his wide face. "Oh man, you're so dead."

DIAMOND IN THE ROUGH
– the "ART" OF DOUG McDOUGAL –

"What!? What!? What does that mean? Doug, what—"

"All right, people, who's next?" Ms. Z tries to smile as at least two dozen hands shoot up instantly. Almost every hand but mine. "You guys can decide this. Whoever's turn it is, that person will come up next, you follow?" We all sit still for a moment, unable to figure out what that meant, until Annie Cantor pops up, walks toward the front of the room with a sheet of rolled-up paper, giggles, turns around, returns to her table, and tries dragging her best, best, best friend, Miranda Waller, to the front of the class with her.

Miranda Waller tries to stay in her seat, mumbles something to Annie, who then instructs Miranda in a loud, friendly, embarrassed whisper to *"Shut UP!"* Annie walks back to the front of the room, stopping three times on her twenty-foot journey in order to turn around and whisper/shout *"Stop!"* at Miranda. Eventually, she unrolls her paper, which contains two long, overlapping streaks of paint, one red, one yellow.

"This is the ketch—"

Annie's uncontrollable laughter. Ms. Z saying, "Take a deep breath" over and over. Annie telling Miranda to shut up. Me wishing that someone with a working brain sat near me. Annie saying, "Okay, okay, okay." Deep inhalation.

"This is the ketchup and mustard that I put in—"

Annie explodes with laughter. In an effort to get herself under control, she covers her face with her painting, makes a loud hooting sound, and then pretty much hyperventilates. The class's laughter changes from the "laughing with" to the "laughing at" variety.

I'm not laughing at all.

Ms. Z walks over to Annie, takes her hand, and says something into her ear. Here's what we've been waiting for:

"This is the ketchup and mustard that I put in—" Annie buries her head in Ms. Z's side and screams, "Jay Bissell's underwear!"

The class cheers loudly.

Ms. Z looks around the room. "Sam Lewis." She points to me.

"Huh?" I wasn't even raising my hand!

A gentle smile. "Your turn to amaze us."

"But—"

"Please, Sam. Sometimes you choose art, but sometimes art chooses you. C'mon, don't be scared to work through it."

So I take my notebook, the one I haven't touched since coming into class, and stand up. The room turns just a bit, first clockwise, then counterclockwise, but I decide this has nothing to do with my friend Tootsie. I wait for the posters all over the walls to stop moving and then slowly walk toward the front of the class.

I look out onto a small sea of yellow T-shirts and blue shorts. You might think that after everything that's already happened today and everything that might still happen, I couldn't possibly care about this, too. But guess what? Turns out I can always find the energy to worry about looking stupid.

I clear my throat. Adjust my shirt collar. Then I ask Ms. Z, "Is a haiku okay?"

"Sure, Sam." Ms. Z smiles softly.

I take a deep breath. This is what comes out:

"Cranium salad

Spaghetti Tripadero

Not all that funny"

But before the class has a chance to respond: the fire alarm.

12:54

I imagine most fire alarms are intended to make you think, *Hmm. What's that loud noise? Huh, I guess there must be a fire nearby. Good thing this alarm is just loud enough to inform me of a fire, but not so loud I can't think clearly at a dangerous time like this.*

But the Wagner Middle School fire alarm is not your good, old-fashioned bell clanger, no sirree. It's a high-pitched, pulsing electronic wail that goes between extremely loud and way louder than extremely loud. During the cruelest section of the alarm's three-part song (which sounds something like *AAAAHHHHHH-OOOOOHHHH-EEEEEEEEE!!!!!!!*), I can feel the blood vessels in Tootsie swell even more. Our fire alarm is so loud that all I can think is: *Must get away from this sound right now.*

It doesn't help that Ms. Z is responsible for our orderly evacuation. While the rest of the class sprints out into the hallway (we're wearing our PE uniforms, ready to run), Ms. Z waves her hands around her head (like the alarm is a very large and very annoying bug buzzing in her ear) and screams, "Go. Go! Just go!!"

Once we get out into the hallway, teachers are yelling things that definitely should not be yelled in a public school, things that wouldn't be allowed in a PG-13 movie. Kids are racing all over the place, running into each other, crashing into walls, banging into lockers. Apparently, everyone has forgotten how to exit the building.

Somehow I soon find myself, without a single one of my classmates in sight, standing out on the blacktop. I'm a bit relieved to be here because of a fire, and not in order to have my butt kicked by Morgan. Also, I know there couldn't possibly be a *real* fire nearby, because when have you ever heard of an actual fire at an actual school? We only have these ridiculous drills so the grown-ups can force us to file out obediently a couple times a year and then lecture us about how our lack of respect could get us killed if this had been a real fire.

I get far enough away from the building for the alarm to become just an irritating siren when I see a bunch of Vikings running toward the west end of the building, near the faculty parking lot. I follow after them, turn a corner, where OMG:

An actual fire.

Okay, it's not really a fire, but there's a broken window with purplish smoke pouring out of it. It's coming from Mr. Rozier's room.

The room where Morgan is supposed to be right now.

A trio of hysterical fire trucks pulls into the parking lot and spits out a bunch of firefighters, dressed and ready for action. Above the din of sirens and alarms, I hear a number of teachers attempting to herd us away from the building and onto the sports field.

The herding is pretty sloppy, since everyone is looking back toward the school. People are bumping into one another, tripping over potholes, tripping over the people who tripped over potholes, tripping over the people who tripped over the people who tripped over the potholes. No one is saying nice things to anyone. I scan the crowd for Morgan and Chris, especially Morgan, but at only fifty-five inches tall, I can't exactly see over the stumbling crowd of blue and yellow.

A loud, glassy pop freezes the crowd momentarily, followed by another, then another. Each pop is answered by a few hundred people shrieking. Then a voice through a megaphone:

"TEACHERS! YOU MUST MOVE YOUR CARS! TEACHERS, MOVE YOUR CARS TO MAKE WAY FOR THE FIRE TRUCKS!"

Just like that, almost all the adults in our mob disappear,

creating a teacher-to-student ratio that is not going to lead to much successful herding. After all, us students aren't much interested in going where we're supposed to go, since the alternative is standing dangerously close to what is now a big-time fire.

I make my way to the edge of the herd and see flames shooting out of the windows of Mr. Rozier's room. Every few seconds a sharp pop, coming from the same direction, makes me jump. The firefighters have a hose on the building, but the fire doesn't seem to care. I can't tell if I'm excited or terrified or stunned or what. Maybe I'm actually all three things, because all I do know is that everyone around me looks like a confused zombie who just drank a Big Gulp of Mountain Dew.

The first three fire trucks have been joined by another two, along with a half dozen ambulances and at least ten police cars. This impressive collection of flashing sirens makes me feel like the carnival has come to town, assuming there's a carnival that also burns down local schools (not a bad idea, now that I think about it).

The alarm (still raging) and the pops are suddenly joined by a dull crash. I turn my head quickly to see that two faculty cars are doing a convincing imitation of Siamese twins joined at the trunks. Mr. Rozier, probably among the least pleased of all the teachers to begin with, jumps out of his car to scream at Ms. Z, who was driving the other car.

"Mika! Are you blind?!" He throws his hands over his head for emphasis.

"Dan, please." Ms. Z holds out a single hand in an effort to hold him back while she collects herself.

"You could have killed me!" Now he's pointing at her.

"C'mon, Dan. I didn't see you." She's looking down at their cars. "Ah, Dan. Look, man, I'm real sorry."

"Sorry? You're sorry?!"

But before we get a chance to learn where this friendly dialogue is headed, a third car, not wanting to be left out, decides to join the twins, and the crash of shattering headlights is added to the other soothing sounds already in the air. Mr. Rozier screams out his most outraged "WHAT?!" so far, but Captain Megaphone interrupts everyone before the identity of Driver Number Three (my money's on Mr. Griegs, even though he's supposed to be at the hospital) can be revealed:

"STUDENTS! MOVE TO THE SPORTS FIELD! NOW! I REPEAT, MOVE TO THE SPORTS FIELD NOW!!"

Captain Megaphone sounds even less happy than Mr. Rozier.

Reluctantly, we do what we're told, herding ourselves in much the same manner as the adults herded us before. More tripping, stumbling, falling, and cursing. Somehow I eventually find myself, along with everyone else, on the Wagner Middle School sports field.

Scanning for familiar faces, I finally locate Amy and am about to call her name when I feel a strong push on my back. I turn around.

Morgan.

He's standing right in front of me, and (along with everyone else, I guess) he doesn't look too happy. "I'm totally gonna kick your butt, Sam."

I look at Morgan and for a moment everything else

around me disappears. The crowd, the sirens, the fire, the purple smoke, that angry voice coming through that megaphone. Just me and Morgan. And for some weird reason, all I can think is: *Well, at least now I know if Morgan decided to forgive me after I decided not to blame him for throwing that salad bowl.*

1:00

"Fight! Fight! Fight!"

You'd think with a real fire nearby, with about twenty emergency vehicles parked outside our school, with a news truck or two having probably shown up by now, and with a three-car pileup tossed into the mix for good measure, my fellow Vikings wouldn't be so interested in what everyone knows will not be much of a fight.

"Fight! Fight! Fight!"

But maybe the lopsided nature of this matchup actually explains everyone's enthusiasm. Maybe they'd all be chanting, *Sam's totally going to get his butt kicked, it's not even going to be close! Sam's totally going to get his butt kicked, it's not even going to be close! Sam's totally going to get his butt kicked, it's not even going to be close!* if that were the kind of thing that made for a good chant. But, of course, it doesn't. So, instead, the old standby:

"Fight! Fight! Fight!"

A large circle (with about twice as much empty space inside it as the one I was at the center of not long ago) has formed around us. Chris, looking as happy as I've ever seen him, stands behind Morgan, egging him on. Morgan is bouncing up and down a little, doing strange things with his hands, which are pretty much fists at this point. Either he's not entirely sure he wants to do this or he simply can't decide exactly how to start hurting me.

I'm really hoping it's the first of those two.

As for me, I'm quickly reviewing my knowledge of self-defense, only to realize all I can come up with is "X-A down," which, yes, is how you assume a defensive stance in Alien Wars. Unfortunately, my knowledge of fighting, until this moment, has been exclusively virtual and two-dimensional.

Welcome to the real, three-dimensional world, Sam.

"Fight! Fight! Fight!"

Morgan comes toward me. I close my eyes and feel two hands hit my chest as I am launched backward through the air. When I open my eyes, I discover that I am no longer standing.

"C'mon, get up!" Morgan orders me.

I'm really not trying to make him any angrier, but sometimes I just can't help myself. "You forgot to say 'please.'"

But rather than correct himself, Morgan instead demonstrates his good manners by coming over and yanking me up. An awfully generous act on his part, if you can ignore the fact that he's helping me up just so he can put me back down again.

"Fight! Fight! Fight!"

"C'mon, Sam." Morgan holds his fists up but doesn't move.

"C'mon what?" I'm not being sarcastic. I really don't know what he could possibly want from me, other than staying somewhere inside our circle of ex-friendship so I can provide his punches with a good target.

For some reason, Morgan lowers his hands. "Take your best shot."

"Yeah!" Chris screams with glee. "Let little Sammy boy have a chance!"

And I actually think about it for a moment. I close my right hand into a fist and take a step toward Morgan, but then something stops me, something other than me knowing that my pathetic punch won't do a thing to Morgan anyway.

I really don't want to punch him. I just don't. So I stand there, hands at my sides.

"Fight! Fight! Fight!"

By the way, this seems like as good a time as any to mention that I am now a big fan of homeschooling.

Morgan says, "C'mon," takes a step closer, and relaunches me across the sports field. I meet the grass with more force this time, and I can't say it feels good. Now I'm actually a little mad.

I look up and see Amy, near whose feet I've just crash-landed. Judging by her horrified expression, I'd say she can't help but root for the losing team, which doesn't make me feel all that much better right now. She bends over and tries to help me up. "Sam, you've got to do something."

I stumble getting up, because I can't even do that right. "Any suggestions?"

But she just backs up a bit and makes one of those "don't ask me" faces.

"Amy," I say as I wipe some of the grass and dirt off my uniform, "I really don't want to sound prejudiced here, but don't you know karate or something?"

But here's Morgan, always ready with a helping hand, dragging me back into Happyland. Amy, thankfully not offended, is pointing at something.

"What?" I yell to her.

She twists her face and keeps pointing to something around waist level, unable to say whatever she's thinking.

"What?" I yell again.

"Fight! Fight! Fight!"

"Kick him in the . . . ," she says, and now I understand what she's pointing at.

Right, of course. My only chance. True, I don't want to punch him, but kicking is another matter altogether.

Morgan is back in his stance, waiting for me. Chris is drooling and/or foaming at the mouth. My fellow Vikings seem not to be having much difficulty choosing between the sacrifice of their MVAT (Most Valuable ArithmeTitan), on the one hand, and a chance to see an unequal fistfight play itself out, on the other. Meanwhile, our school is, last I checked, on fire. Whatever was popping continues to pop. A new sound from directly overhead alerts me to the fact that the pilot of the Channel 2 News Chopper might also have the pleasure of watching me get beat up. Who knows, if the fire is already under control, they might even film us. What a way to make the six o'clock news.

With exactly one good idea to my name in this situation, I let out what I believe is a pretty solid battle cry (something

along the lines of: "YEEAAGHHHGHGHGAAAAHHH!!!"),
rush toward Morgan, close my eyes, plant my left foot, and
kick hard with my right, as I picture him grasping a certain
very sensitive region in agony—

SEVENTH GRADER OF STEEL
A SUBSTANCE-BY-SUBSTANCE GUIDE TO MORGAN STURTZ

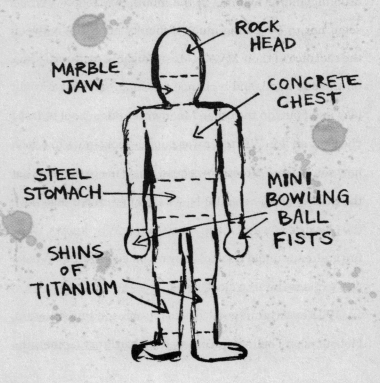

ROCK HEAD

MARBLE JAW

CONCRETE CHEST

STEEL STOMACH

MINI BOWLING BALL FISTS

SHINS OF TITANIUM

But this is real life, so why would my foot perform better than normal? I miscalculate my blow entirely, hit his upper shin, and, I'm 99 percent certain, break between three and five bones in the top of my foot.

"Ooowww!!!!!" That's me, by the way.

Morgan rubs his lower leg like a small dog just softly bumped into it, while I hop up and down on my left foot, wishing our PE uniforms came with steel-toed boots.

Of course, the sympathy-free circle of Vikings finds all this hilarious. No one ever laughs at my jokes in class. But this? LOL.

I set my bad foot down as another idea comes to me. I run (okay, limp) at Morgan, because if I hug him, maybe he'll remember we used to be friends. Or maybe, at least, he'll have a harder time putting everything he's got into his punches.

The crowd screams in approval, but soon I find myself on the business end of a really impressive headlock. He's squeezing the sides of my precious brain quite hard, and all I can think is: *Not Tootsie, anywhere but Tootsie. Kidneys, fine. Liver, no problem. Just leave poor Tootsie alone.*

And you might think I'm biased here, seeing how Morgan is trying to beat me up and all, but trust me when I say that he really ought to consider switching brands of deodorant (assuming he's using any in the first place).

He starts whispering something angrily. "Why did you write I'm stupid?" And then an extra squeeze. "Why?!"

"I'm sorry." The most honest, sincere thing I've ever said in my entire life, by the way. "I'm really sorry."

More whispering. "Why did you tell Mr. Griegs I used to cheat off you?"

"What?!" I think I heard him right, but this makes no sense. "I never said that!"

"Why did you tell Emma Jacobs I think she's ugly?" Now he's really mad, or really madder.

"What?!" I do not like where this conversation seems to be headed. "I didn't—"

"And why did you tell Keith Lopez that I think he sucks as QB?" Morgan does think Keith Lopez is a subpar quarterback, but no way in the world would I tell Keith this (and that's assuming Keith would even agree to listen to me in the first place).

I'm now more confused than terrified (and I'm *extremely* terrified), but somehow I'm almost comforted to know we're talking again. Okay, I'm not. Not at all. Because now I finally get it; Morgan really hates me, which is way worse than him just hitting me.

"I didn't say any of those things!" I tell his rib cage.

"Liar!" He squeezes harder, like I might not realize he's upset. "You did!"

The crowd has begun to lose its patience. I'm so bad at fighting that I'm not only losing, I'm getting booed, too. Morgan releases me, pushing me back to my end of the circle.

"You're a *liar!*" He points at me as he spits out this last word while his eyes close a bit and his mouth bends down into that strange shape it made last summer, when his mom screamed at him in front of me after we had a water fight in their kitchen (which I'll admit was not one of my better ideas).

"I'm not!" I try sounding as sincere as possible while

still scanning the ground around us for holes big enough for me but too small for him. "I didn't say any of those things."

"He's lying!" Chris yells. "He's a liar!"

In my effort to clear the air, I say something that maybe isn't so smart, but what can I do—the noises coming from every direction combined with the look Morgan is giving me are starting to make my tongue misfire. Speaking pretty loudly across the circle, I tell him, "I only wrote that you were stupid."

The crowd, first chanting, then booing, now starts laughing. I can't believe I'm thinking this, but where is Mr. Griegs when you need him?

"What?!" he says. I can't quite tell if he heard me or not, if he's confused and furious or just furious.

"In that note . . ." I know I need to concentrate here and not say the wrong thing, but it feels like sparks are shooting out of Tootsie, like my brain is about to shut down. "The one you saw by accident. I just, I didn't, I just wrote that you're dumb, but—"

Only that's enough for Morgan. With a little push in the back from Chris, he heads my way and finally gives the mob what they've been waiting for all this time. I even see it coming, but it comes too fast. Or could it be I actually think I deserve it? Or, even worse, do I think he'll want to make up now that he's finally gotten this out of his system?

All I know is that it comes fast and it comes hard. His fist, my face. Horrible combination. The exact opposite of chocolate and peanut butter.

I'm on the ground (again), feeling like my mouth is now directly below my right ear. The crowd celebrates for a few seconds while I wait to visit la-la land for the second time this afternoon. But somehow I don't. I close my eyes for a moment and feel my jaw replace Tootsie as the King of Throbbing. When I open them up again, I see Amy, who looks so upset that I almost feel worse for her than I do for myself. Much to my amazement, I somehow stand back up and look over at Morgan, who seems pretty surprised I'm not trying to squeeze my way out of the circle.

"He wants more!" Chris yells. "Yeah! Give it to him!"

And even though part of me still wishes we were MorSam, right now Morgan pretty much looks like just another kid to me. Another mean kid who makes this the worst school ever. Maybe it's only because my head is spinning, but I almost wonder if we ever were friends in the first place.

I start running straight at Morgan. He raises his fists, so I go for his legs. This time I'm going to tackle him, just like I *didn't* do back in my living room. Because then I was only playing nice, trying to give him a little extra confidence. I jump through the air, hit his body, wrap my short arms around his giant legs, and feel him fall with me down to the ground. My popularity with my schoolmates gets a big boost, but they're probably just happy because the fight isn't over after all. Sure enough, Wagner Middle School's starting running back (who I just tackled all by myself, thank you very much) is soon on top of me, pinning my arms under his legs, getting ready to spin my mouth around toward the other ear, when a familiar voice breaks through the circle.

"Stop! Stop that this instant! Get off him!!"

Morgan suddenly lifts up off me, carried away by a force much too strong to belong to anyone I know. I lift my head and see Mr. Glassner (still in his double-breasted blazer, his eyes wide with fury, his angry mouth screaming, "Enough! Enough! Enough!") raise Morgan up and nearly over his head. Morgan squirms in midair, held tight in what I never before realized are Mr. Glassner's powerful hands. My teacher's eyes continue opening wider and wider as his grip tightens, and it looks like he's getting ready to launch Morgan right over Wagner Middle School. But then, at the last second, Ms. Z breaks into the circle and calls out, "Paul, don't! Paul, stop! Stop!!"

Mr. Glassner freezes. His face seems to remember who he is and where we are. Before they shrink back down to normal size, his eyes look right at me, and I swear he's trying to apologize, even though he just saved me and my butt. A split second before Ms. Z pulls me in toward her chest, Mr. Glassner sets my onetime best friend back down again, but he keeps a hand wrapped firmly around Morgan's upper arm. And even after my head is surrounded by Ms. Z's arms, her scarf, and her long, frizzy hair, I can still hear the school alarm wailing, because, well, who knows why. Who knows why anything ever happens the way it happens in this crazy place.

1:11

"You okay, buddy?" Ms. Z asks after she lets go of me.

They must have finally turned the alarm off, because I'm pretty sure that's just an echo in my head.

"Let's see what we got here," Ms. Z says, softly lifting up my chin with the tip of her green-and-purple index finger. We're still sitting on the sports field, only now it's just the two of us. My back is to the school, but I can picture everyone being herded inside, assuming the school isn't a giant pile of ashes by now. I think about turning around to make sure, but something stops me.

"Oh boy," Ms. Z announces, tilting her head to inspect my jaw, "we ought to get you some ice."

Over her shoulder I can see out toward all the houses that border the school. A bunch of trees in their yards are covered in white flowers. The sun is shining. The grass all around us is really green. My mom would look at all this and say, "Wow, what a day for a picnic."

PLANNING A POST-FIGHT PICNIC?

HERE'S WHAT TO PACK!

(YOU'LL HAVE → ☐ FOOD
NO APPETITE,
TRUST ME.) ☒ ROOT BEER
(BUT YOU MIGHT
BE THIRSTY.)

FIRST AID

☒ BLANKET
☒ ICE PACK
☒ YOUR SHAME
(PACKS ITSELF.)

(BRUISED APPLE
THAT UNDERSTANDS
WHERE YOU'RE
COMING FROM)

☒ BAND-AIDS
☒ ASPIRIN

"You feel like standing up?" Ms. Z asks.

I can hear voices over by the school. Probably my fellow Vikings, half of them twisting their heads all the way around to see if I'm crying or bleeding (or both), and all of them reviewing the fight and agreeing it was pretty awesome.

"Can you stand up?" Ms. Z tries again.

"Yes," I say, and not very nicely.

"Great. Let me help you up." She stands first, brushes herself off, and then offers me a hand.

"I can do it myself." Which I can, though the fact that my jaw is no longer symmetrical messes up my balance a bit.

"You okay?"

A plane, on its way to who knows where, draws out a thin white line. Even if it were being flown by a blind ape, I'd be happy to be on it right now.

"Why don't we go back to the school? Nurse Landen should probably have a look at your jaw."

Planes make clouds because of their exhaust.

"Sam." Ms. Z puts a hand on my shoulder. "How about we go back?"

I look up at Ms. Z, who's trying to smile. Which means her mouth is smiling, sort of, but not the rest of her.

"Look, Sam." She shakes her head slowly. "I'm sorry about this. I'm really sorry. You got a raw deal today."

I agree with her, but for some reason this isn't making me feel better. Not at all.

"But, you know, now it's over." She smiles again, for real this time, or at least half of her face smiles for real. "Now you get to move on."

"Move on?" I hate it when people are stupid. I hate it even more when smart people are stupid. I turn and start walking toward the school, but there's still a handful of students and teachers who haven't filed back inside yet. A bunch of the police cars are gone, and the firefighters are done watering our school. No smoke and no popping anymore either.

"Well, I don't know," Ms. Z says, and pulls up next to me so that the two of us can stare at Wagner Middle School together. "Sometimes you dread something. Convince yourself you'll die if it happens. And then it happens. But guess what? You don't die. And not only don't you die, but once it's over you can stop worrying about it."

I start walking very, very slowly to the school. Not because I want to. Because now that "it's over" I've got so much to look forward to: walking around with a giant bruise on my face that reminds everyone who won the Morgan-Sam battle, having exactly no friends, and watching my ex-friends from halfway across the cafeteria while they sit around and laugh about the fact that I have more bruises on my face than friends in my life. Sure, it's over. Everything's over.

We slowly walk toward the school together without talking. I almost want to thank Ms. Z for being quiet, for being smart enough to know there's no point in trying to cheer me up. Until out of the corner of my eye I notice her stopping.

"Sam," she says.

I don't respond.

"Sam," she repeats herself, this time almost firmly.

I don't even stop walking.

"C'mon, Lewis, seriously," she says, sounding low on patience.

We're already on the blacktop. Fifteen more seconds and we would be inside. "What?" I stop and ask, but not because I'm interested.

Ms. Z catches back up, looks at me, looks away, looks back at me, bites the corner of her mouth, inhales, exhales, but doesn't say a word.

"What?"

"You're right," she finally says, staring straight at me. "This sucks. This sucks in a major, major, *major* way. And you know what else? Middle school, it pretty much sucks too. And I speak from experience. I mean, you've only been here for two years. This is my thirteenth year. Thir-*teen*, Sam. So, you know, I've seen some nasty stuff."

Ms. Z trails off. Looks over toward the fire trucks, maybe at her smashed-up car.

"Yeah, so?" I ask.

"So. So that's the deal, which"—she raises her eyebrows—"you probably already knew. And, well, so here's my advice, and a promise, too: Wait. Be patient. You're not going to be here forever. And in the meantime, even though you and this place don't fit together so great all the time, be you. Morgan and the other guys might not approve, but other people do and—"

"Like who?"

"Who?" Ms. Z asks me right back, confused.

"Yeah, what other people are you talking about?"

She doesn't say anything.

"Seriously." I can feel the parts of my face that weren't already red turning red. "Who approves? Tell me that"—I cross my arms—"Ms. Zuckerman."

Ms. Z closes her eyes. She doesn't blink, she closes her eyes. For what seems like a really long time. Then she removes her glasses, wipes her eyes with one of her baggy sleeves, and, I think, sniffles. When she opens her eyes back up and I see them without her glasses, they're bigger and greener than they've ever been before. I can barely look at them they're so big.

"I do, Sam," she says. "I approve. I do. And I know there are other kids who do too, even if this"—she points at the building—"this *stupid* place makes it hard for them to admit it. So, I don't know, be nice to the ones who are willing to admit it. Because that's all you can do. That's it." Ms. Z puts her glasses back on, sniffles again, turns back to the school, and walks the rest of the way to the building, all by herself, because for some reason I can't move.

1:19

"How do you feel, son?" Principal Benson asks from
the side of his desk. Not only has he brought his chair around
to sit closer to me and Morgan, his legs are crossed as well.
Maybe this is what you learn in principal school: where and
how to sit for a postfight conversation.

"I'm okay," I tell him, or Morgan.

"Samuel"—Principal Benson uncrosses and recrosses
his legs the opposite way—"do you know what our number

one responsibility is here at Wagner Middle School?"

I just shake my head, because I really don't feel like having this or any other conversation with Principal Benson right now, especially with Morgan sitting right next to me.

"You might believe it is to educate you, but, as vital as that task is, it is not. No, our number one responsibility is your safety." He pauses for a moment, because I guess he wants to be sure I'm surprised. Fine, I'm a little surprised. Get on with it already. "And we failed to meet that responsibility today. For that reason"—another pause, who knows why—"I would like to apologize to you personally. You have my word we will never allow such a thing to happen to you again. No, sir. Not on my watch."

"Okay," I say, because now he's clearly waiting for me to say something. "Thanks."

"Of course, Samuel, I'm not the only person here who is sorry." Principal Benson smiles a bit and turns his head to Morgan. Then some silence of the awkward variety, until: "Morgan, is there anything you want to tell your friend?"

Morgan clears his throat, mumbles something.

ROUNDING OUT THE TOP FIVE
·OR· WHAT PRINCIPAL BENSON
THINKS THEY'RE RESPONSIBLE FOR:

#1 OUR SAFETY

#2 OUR EDUCATION

#3 OUR BOREDOM
(FOR AT LEAST EIGHT HOURS A DAY)

#4 OUR CHANCE TO WONDER WHY
WE WEREN'T BORN IN FRANCE
WHERE MAYBE THINGS ARE
DIFFERENT.

#5 OUR OPPORTUNITY TO LOOK
FORWARD TO HIGH SCHOOL,
BECAUSE HOW COULD THAT
POSSIBLY BE ANY WORSE
          THAN THIS?

Principal Benson blinks his eyes a few times. He may

have also just clenched his jaw underneath all that facial

hair. "Morgan, I am going to ask you to repeat whatever you just said. This time, however, I ask that you speak more clearly. I would also ask you to think about what it truly means to say what you're saying. And, Samuel, if you would like, you may look at Morgan so you can know that he means what he says."

I try turning my head, but I can't. And not because my jaw hurts. I settle on my shoe instead.

"I'm sorry." There's an outside chance he might actually have meant it.

"Thank you, Morgan. Samuel, I asked you in here so you can hear, right from the very top, how we're dealing with what happened to you today. Normally, both participants in a physical altercation such as this would receive a suspension, but according to numerous eyewitnesses, you did not initiate this altercation, nor did you have a reasonable opportunity to defuse it. So you are, as they say, off the hook. Morgan, on the other hand, should be looking at an extended suspension. However, because he provided us with crucial information regarding the origins of the fire"—I look up from my shoe at Principal Benson—"because Morgan has done this, Morgan will be allowed to return to school in two weeks' time."

"What information?" I ask.

"I am sorry, Samuel," Principal Benson says, not looking all that sorry to me, "but I am not at liberty to disclose those details at this time."

"That's totally stupid," I say, before I realize what I'm saying. But Principal Benson doesn't respond. "I'm sorry." And then I try to shut up, but I think I still mumble, "but it is."

"Samuel," Principal Benson says, and he may be trying to smile, who knows why, "I understand your frustration, but I ask you to try to understand the demands of protocol in this situation. There are reports to be filed, parents to be informed, and various state agencies to be contacted. You will learn all that you need to learn in good time."

"State agencies?" I try turning toward Morgan again, but my head won't allow it. Back to my shoe. "Where's Chris?"

Principal Benson examines his fingernails. "Chris Tripadero will not be returning to Wagner Middle School." More silence.

With Chris gone, even after all this, maybe, who knows?

"Gentlemen," Principal Benson chimes in again, "today's events got me thinking about a little saying I try to live by. Would you like to hear it?"

We both say, "Sure." Politely, not enthusiastically.

"What is so fascinating about this saying is that despite its profundity, it contains no word more than two letters long." He looks at us, wanting to see if this little factoid has impressed us. Sure, I'm impressed. "Here it is, ten words." And he lifts up both hands to count them off with his fingers. *"If it is to be, it is up to me."* A smile of deep satisfaction. "I think you'll agree that—"

A knock at the door. Principal Benson says, "Excuse me for a moment," stands, buttons his suit jacket, and opens the door just a crack. "Hello . . . Principal Benson . . . Yes . . . Thank you for coming." He closes the door and speaks to us. "Gentlemen, I need to speak confidentially with these good people out here in the hall for a moment. I trust you are both aware that any poor decisions you might make while I'm standing just on the other side of this door will be dealt with most severely." I nod. I assume Morgan does the same.

Soon it's just me, Morgan, and my shoe.

1:23

"What'd you tell them?" I stare at my shoe and ask him.

"That Chris started the fire," Morgan mumbles.

"How do you know?" Soon I'll actually look at Morgan.

"I saw it," he says, a little more clearly.

"They believe you?"

"He sent me a couple e-mails, like a month ago," Morgan says, like e-mail is the dumbest thing ever, "explaining how he'd do it. Said he was definitely going to at some point."

I try looking at him but only make it halfway through my sentence. "How did he do it?"

"Mr. Rozier left a cabinet unlocked with a bunch of chemicals in it near our lab station. Plus, there was a trash can right there. Chris put his dirty clothes in the can, poured some chemical on it, dropped a match in." Morgan sounds like he's reading out loud the most uninteresting recipe in the history of cooking.

"So why today?" I ask, but Morgan just shrugs. "Was it so he could get us both outside?" But Morgan doesn't say anything. "And why'd you tell them?" I ask, looking down at my other shoe for a change. Morgan doesn't answer. "You got Chris kicked out of school."

"Chris does too much stupid stuff," Morgan says, sounding like he just figured this out for the very first time. It almost makes me feel better, and I look at him so he can see I agree, but he's staring straight ahead at the Viking Code. "Benson said Coach might suspend me for the first two games next year. Said he probably will—said he's considering four games. Chris, man, he doesn't care about anything."

I can hear three voices, two male and one female, on the other side of the door, but I can't make out any of the words they're saying. But still, the voices are pretty clear, almost familiar.

"You know I didn't say any of that stuff," I tell him, trying to sound like I don't care whether or not he knows this.

"So?" Of course he's better than me at sounding like he doesn't care.

"So"—eyes back on my shoe—"so, I didn't say any of it. And I didn't mean to give that note to anyone. I didn't even mean what I wrote in it."

"So?"

I turn back to him, determined not to look away, fighting to keep my jaw from shaking, which, yes, hurts a lot, a lot more than Tootsie ever hurt. "Chris was just trying to get us to fight."

Morgan must really find that poster interesting, because he won't stop looking at it. It's like he's hanging on to the thing for dear life. Well, of course he is. Morgan will die if he can't play. Football might be stupid, but it sure makes Morgan happy, so happy that, I don't know, maybe it's not so stupid after all. And if we—or if I—I mean, if he can't play because of something I did. That note and me showing off all those times until he actually let Chris convince him to fight me. Because if he's not allowed to wear his jersey on game day, and if I had anything to do with it, even just a small part—or maybe a medium part, actually—I don't know what I'll do.

But I could make it up to him if he'll let me.

"You know," I tell him, or at least his shoes, "we could, you know, still hang out and stuff. Now that Chris is gone."

Morgan drags his feet under his chair, so I lift up my head and notice the red marks on his right hand. The damage my jaw did to his fist.

Then he makes a sound like a laugh. Like this is funny. Like this whole thing is totally hilarious.

The room is silent. But I can still hear his laugh. I can hear it louder and clearer than when it first happened, until suddenly, the last thing on my mind is Morgan and his jersey. I turn away from him, listen to those voices on the other side of the door, and sit like I'd sit if it were just me in here, alone, waiting for Principal Benson to come back.

Morgan's going to be gone for two weeks. Chris will be gone even longer. Two weeks to figure out where to sit at lunch.

The door opens, this time all the way. Morgan's parents, Edward and Jocelyn, are standing next to Principal Benson. They do not look very happy. Only his mom seems to notice me, and that's just for a split second. Even though I ate dinner at their kitchen table a couple times a month since I was six.

"Let's go, Morgan," his dad announces.

But before Morgan is done standing up, Principal Benson suddenly closes the door. The voices start up again, only this time I can make out more than three. And the new voices, two of them, are way, way more familiar than the ones belonging to Morgan's parents. I still can't hear their actual words, but I know their tones so well I can figure out exactly what they're saying.

My dad: Is Sam in there?

My mom: Is he okay? Are you sure?

Which means that my mom came back from St. Louis early. Even before she heard what happened. Which means she missed me. A lot. Plus my dad dropped everything to come here, even though my mom obviously could have picked me up all by herself.

I think the vibrations of their voices aren't just passing through the door, they're passing straight into me. Because why else would I be shaking like this?

Morgan, who froze for a moment or two when the door closed again, takes a step toward it. Even though he was probably trying to avoid it, his eyes look at me for a moment. At which point I start shaking for real and can feel things happening up around my own eyes. This can't happen right now. Getting beaten up is one thing, but there's no way I'm going to let him see me cry, too.

So I do something I saw in a movie or read in a book or maybe just make up right here on the spot: I bite the inside of my lip. I bite it hard, so it will hurt, so that it will hurt enough to short-circuit all the other stuff, the shaking that won't stop and the tears that seem determined to find their way out. For a moment or two I'm not sure it's going to work, so I bite even harder, clenching my swollen jaw, feeling the inside of my lip as I crush it between my teeth. I bite harder, until it hurts more than anything else has hurt today, until I need to close my eyes and breathe in all the air inside the office, until I can feel the room start to tilt and flip all the way around.

1:27:52 TO 1:27:59

nce upon a time there was a boy named Sam Lewis, and one day he and his ex–best friend, Morgan Sturtz, are sitting in the office because they got in a fight. Sam's and Morgan's parents are waiting right outside the door, and, when the principal opens the door, all four parents flood into the office.

Actually, **O**nce upon a time Morgan leaves first, and a few seconds later he and his parents disappear forever. Then Sam goes outside and hugs his parents.

No, actually, Once upon a time, right after Morgan and his parents disappear forever, Sam's parents see their son's jaw before they even hug him. So they look at Principal Benson like he's the one who did it, and he apologizes again and really means it this time. Then Sam's mom hugs her son for almost one entire minute, until Sam's dad says, "C'mon, Becca, let's go."

So the three of them start walking out of the school, which smells like burnt eggs, only to run into Mr. Glassner, who smiles, shakes Sam's parents' hands, and apologizes as well. "Truly regrettable what happened today," Mr. Glassner says, "but perhaps not all is lost." Sam and his parents, all quite puzzled, look at Mr. Glassner, so he explains: "I was able to get today's meet rescheduled to take place at E. C. Dunbar. Might Sam, despite all that happened today, still be willing to take on the vaunted CalcuLeaders in less than one hour? Normally, I'd allow this event to, as it were, go up in smoke, but in light of today's special celebrity judge, well, I was very much hoping not to have to cancel."

Of course, the only problem is that almost all the

other students have already left, because school was canceled, because school was recently on fire. And as anyone who knows the first thing about the rules of the Michigan Matholympics Association can tell you, each team at a meet must field at least three competitors or be forced to forfeit. Mr. Glassner, knowing these rules by heart, informs them, "I was able to locate Elliot Baumgarten." Sam tries not to laugh, and Mr. Glassner says, his eyes shrinking with a smile of his own, "I'll admit he's not exactly first-string material, but if we field a solid one and two, we should be fine."

"But who is going to be our number two?" Sam asks.

So they begin searching the school, and a couple minutes later, who do they find? None other than Amy Takahara, studying Latin prefixes, waiting for her parents to pick her up, and worrying about Sam. At first she's not willing to compete, but after Sam offers to help her study Greek suffixes later that evening, she agrees. And they all go to Dunbar, where Sam performs so brilliantly that even the losing CalcuLeaders join in the applause. As soon as the clapping dies down, Professor Davies, the totally bald celebrity judge, rushes up to Sam and says, "Highly impressive. You've got a bright, bright future ahead of you." And he is right, because afterward they all go out to pizza, and Amy and Sam sit together at lunch every day from that moment on.

Actually, once upon a time Amy and Sam eat lunch together every day from that moment on, until mid-October in eighth grade, when Amy's dad gets a new job and she has to move again, this time to Orlando, Florida. So, after almost six months of living happily ever after, Sam is a lonely loser once more. He sits all alone in the cafeteria and watches Morgan, captain of the football team and most popular kid in school, eat lunch with all their old friends and perhaps even with a couple girls as well, since eighth graders, especially the cool ones, always seem to have girlfriends.

Or, no, once upon a time Sam is a lonely loser again, but only for a little while, because around Thanksgiving he makes a new friend, maybe even two new friends—well, he makes at least one, some new kid with curly hair named

Darren, who shares his Ho Hos with Sam most days.

Sometimes Sam and Morgan pass each other in the hall, and because the two of them are so definitely not friends by this point, Morgan doesn't even bother ignoring Sam anymore. Sam might as well just be any other kid at school. Every once in a while Sam hears some news or rumor about Morgan: that he was asked to work out with the high school team, that he bench-pressed two hundred pounds, that he's going out with Kelly Davidson, who is almost certainly going to be a supermodel one day. Sam is interested in this news, but not too much.

Then, in the final term of eighth grade, Sam and Morgan get stuck in the same cooking class together, even though neither of them signed up for it. They'll even wind up getting put in the same cooking group. At first it will be super awkward, but then it will gradually start to feel normal (and will be kind of fun, too, especially the red velvet cake disaster), until, well, the two won't exactly become friends again, but when they take that picture together, just the two of them, right after middle school graduation in June, each of them wearing a graduation robe and a tassled cap, they will both be smiling for the same reason. Because even if a friendship like MorSam comes to an end, it can never end completely.

Actually, nce upon a time, Sam Lewis and Morgan Sturtz were best friends. Then they stopped being friends. And for better or for worse, they were never friends again. But they were best friends, for a bunch of years they were definitely best friends. They were maybe even the very best friend either of them would ever have.

The end, probably.

1:28

I open my eyes, let go of my lip, and feel the room turn back to its normal position. Morgan, probably standing the whole time, stares at me like I'm a creature from another planet, but he doesn't say anything. Instead, he takes a couple steps toward the door, toward all those voices that are still talking.

"Hey, Morgan," I say.

He stops, right next to the side of Principal Benson's

desk, but doesn't bother looking at me. "What?"

"Morgan," I calmly say his name again.

Now he turns around, more than a little annoyed. "What?"

This time I look right at him, my eyes no longer dragged down to my shoes or his. I wait a second, because I want to make sure he's listening.

My mouth and jaw still hurt, but I have no problem saying the word as clearly as I've ever heard anyone ever say it: "Good-bye."

FABLEHAVEN

FROM *NEW YORK TIMES*
BESTSELLING AUTHOR

Brandon Mull

FROM ALADDIN   KIDS.SIMONANDSCHUSTER.COM